بسم الله الرحمن الرحيم

Sophia's Journal

NAJIYAH DIANA MAXFIELD

DAYBREAK PRESS
2014

Sophia's Journal was originally published in 2008 by Muslim Writers Publishing, under the title *Sophia's Journal: Time Warp 1857*

Published by:
Daybreak Press
St. Paul, Minnesota, USA

Library of Congress Catalog Control Number: 2007943041

ISBN: 978-0-9906259-0-2

Cover illustration by Azra Momin
Edited by Maysan Haydar
Book design and typesetting by scholarlytype.com

Printed in the United States of America

For the Shaykhah

And

In loving memory of Jamilah Kolocotronis Jitmoud, who gave of herself with love to her family, with wisdom for her students and with support for my endeavors. Sophia owes everything to you

May Allah forgive your shortcomings,
increase your rank,
and
reward your family,
Ameen.

Acknowledgments

I testify that there is no god but Allah, and that Muhammad was His last messenger. All praise and thanks is due to Allah, may He shower His blessings and peace upon our beloved Prophet.

Special thanks to my husband Bassam, who is an urban man to the core - except for his heart of hearts, which is prairie all the way. And to my kids: Waheeb, Amani, Jenan, Sarah, Hisham and Ibrahim, whose faith in me is an inestimable blessing.

And finally to Anse Tamara Gray, who focuses the light on our path. May Allah bless all your visions and make each and every one a reality. The leper would know you in an instant.

SOPHIA WAS GLAD HER parents had planned the biking trip. It meant she didn't have to search around for an excuse.

"Come on, Soph! We're going to spend tomorrow night at Sarah's and stay up all night watching movies. It'll be fun!" coaxed her best friend Amani.

"Yeah!" added Jenan, waving her pita bread in her effort to convince Sophia to come, dripping some hummus dip on her blue headscarf in the process. "Sarah's brother's going to be at baseball camp in Lawrence."

Sarah nodded, affirming the news that her eighteen-year-old brother would be out of the house.

". . .so we'll have the whole basement to ourselves and even *my* parents said I could go. It's a once-in-a-lifetime chance!" Jenan was a year younger than the other girls, but the ninth and tenth grades were combined at their small Islamic school, so they were all in the same class.

The girls were eating hummus, an Arabic bean dip, and pita bread at the Damascus Café, which had become their favorite hangout since Jenan's dad had opened it the year before. It wasn't that Sophia didn't want to be with her friends. She did. She loved watching movies with her friends, and Sarah's mom, Sr. Azza, was the coolest. She was a great cook and she joked along with the girls. It was just that Sophia could never bring herself to sleep away from home. The last time she'd tried had been in the eighth grade, when she'd been invited to spend the night by the new girl, Huda. Everything had been fine until it got dark and Huda's mom went to bed. Then Sophia had thrown up pizza and hot Cheetos (at least she'd made it to the bathroom!). She'd lain in bed for two hours, trying to conquer her terror and fall back to sleep.

But they were on the second floor! What if there were a fire? Had Huda's family practiced escape routes? Could she and Huda reach the backyard tree from the window? Sophia had gotten up to check. It was pretty close. They could probably make it if they had to.

Sophia had lain back down and tried to convince herself that her fears had been assuaged. And they actually had been. . .until she remembered that Huda's neighbors had a huge yard with a dog and a small flock of chickens in their backyard. Sophia began to wonder how close you had to get to a chicken to catch bird flu from it.

Then she heard a siren. What if it was going to her house? What if that little pain in her leg was a blood clot or something and it traveled to her brain? Then *she'd* need an ambulance!

Sophia had set about breathing slowly and making *dhikr* and *du'a* like her mom had taught her, and that helped. For about ten minutes. Finally, ready to throw up a second time, Sophia had called her parents. It was 2 am. She pretended she had the flu and everyone felt sorry for her. Little did they know it was really the bird flu (and the fire escape route, and the possible blood clot) that had made her sick.

Of course, not all of Sophia's fears were that outlandish. She worried about regular things like tests and her complexion, but she also worried about crazy things. In the fourth grade, when they'd had tornado drills at school, she'd worried for weeks afterward that a tornado was going to come in the middle of the night and kill everyone she knew. She'd once heard a newswoman say that terrorists might get hold of a nuclear weapon. That had cost her about a month of restful sleep.

Her mom, who was from a small town, and who'd told Sophia that she had also worried a lot when she was younger, advised her to pray about her worries, and she did. It helped some—Sophia wasn't as much of a head case as she had been in the eighth grade when she'd spent the night at Huda's—but worried thoughts still intruded on her days. As a Muslim, she firmly believed that God is in charge of things and that nothing can happen to a person that is not His will. But she also knew that sometimes His will involves tests and trials, and those can be scary and painful. When she was six, she'd been stung by a bee. Her throat had swollen up and she'd almost gone into anaphylactic shock. It was terrifying. So even though Sophia knew that Allah promises ease after hardship, and even though she knew that the chances of her catching malaria or dying in a house fire were very remote, those facts didn't alleviate her fears; they came, un-bidden.

So Sophia was glad to be able to tell her friends that her parents had planned a family biking trip that Memorial Day weekend.

Amani called her later that night. After the usual hunt for her phone, Sophia found it on the bookcase and answered just before the voicemail picked up.

"Are you really going biking?" Amani asked, "Or are you just you-know-what?"

Amani had been Sophia's best friend since preschool. The girls knew each other inside and out. One of the reasons Sophia liked Amani so much was that even though she didn't appear to be afraid of anything herself, she didn't give Sophia a hard time about her phobias. And she never teased her in front of other people. Of course, Sophia also knew about the time in second grade when two of the neighbor girls had held Amani down and tickled her until she peed her pants, and Sophia never brought that up in front of others either.

"Yeah, we are," Sophia answered. "My dad's still on his health and fitness kick, remember? He wants to ride the bikes along the Kansas River trail from DeSoto to Lawrence Saturday, spend the night in Lawrence with my cousins, and then ride back along the river Sunday."

Sophia's father, who fondly remembered a childhood of riding his bike all over Damascus, Syria, had bought everyone mountain bikes for Eid—Sophia, her parents, and her little brother Hisham, who was a year younger than Sophia but not actually littler than she was anymore. He'd been towering over her since seventh grade.

"Aren't you worried the trail will be crowded? Everyone and their brother will be camping this weekend." Crowds were another thing that bothered Sophia.

"Actually, I don't mind crowds outdoors. It's when I'm closed in with a lot of people that I get weird. Anyway, my dad says this trail's 'off the beaten path.' He and Mom went to college in Lawrence so he knows the area. What I'm most worried about is sore legs and a numb behind, after all that riding." Sophia laughed.

"Well, OK. If you're sure you're not just copping out on us," Amani said.

"I'm sure."

"Alright. When are you coming back?"

"Sunday afternoon sometime, *insha'Allah*. Dad's got a Tuesday deadline for some big story." Sophia's dad was a reporter for the *Kansas City Star*.

"Call me when you get in, OK? I'll save you some junk food from the party if I can."

"Alright, thanks. *AsSalaamu Alaikum*." "*Wa Alaikum AsSalaam*."

When the girls hung up, Sophia flung the phone onto the couch and went to her room to pack.

"*SubhanAllah!*" shouted her parrot, Kuzko, when she entered. "*Wa Alhamdulillah!*" she answered, smiling. Her dad had brought her the little green Quaker Parrot when he'd been in Texas the year before. He was safe from bird flu because he always stayed indoors. When they'd gotten him, he'd only said two things: "Hey baaaaby" and "shut up." She'd been trying to teach him something in Arabic for months, but *AsSalaamu Alaikum*, the Muslim greeting, seemed a bit more than Kuzko could manage. So she'd been saying, "*SubhanAllah*" (praise God) whenever she entered her room. Now he thought *SubhanAllah* was a greeting and said it whenever he saw anyone. He still said "shut up" sometimes, too, though.

Sophia took the remaining school books out of her new backpack. What a great feeling, to finally

6

be able to take them out for the last time. She considered using her ratty old nylon book bag for the trip, in case she fell in the mud or something, but decided against it. She wasn't sure where it was and she loved her new one too much to leave it behind. It was real leather and held a lot. She'd gotten it for $18 when Skins, the leather store at the mall, had gone out of business. She left the pencils and change in the outside pocket but emptied out the rest of it. She put the books on the top shelf of her closet and turned her attention to packing.

Packing for an overnight trip, especially when she was going to be outdoors, was not exactly a simple thing for Sophia. Hisham just threw a pair of clean boxers, his toothbrush, and his Gameboy into his bag and he was ready to go. Sophia needed a lot more stuff than that. Anyone would think she was going on a month-long safari, the way she packed.

When her bag was finally ready, she took Kuzko out of his cage and into the family room. Her mom was folding laundry and she asked Sophia to put it away. Sophia hated putting away laundry. Hisham had just come in from mowing the lawn and was sitting sideways in the big chair, watching a baseball game on TV.

"I'm not putting Hisham's stuff away," Sophia declared.

"That's fine," said her mother. "He can do his own." She missed Hisham's mocking face, imitating Sophia behind her back. Kuzko didn't miss it, though.

"Shut up!" he squawked.

THE NEXT MORNING DAWNED cloudy and warm, with a slight breeze but no forecast of rain. That was more of a blessing than usual, as it had rained a lot that spring.

Twice Brush Creek, which usually wound lazily through Kansas City, had overstepped its banks and poured into the streets downtown. Flash floods were not unusual in the area, normally occurring three or four times a year, but these were worse than previous years because the creeks and rivers were already swollen from a very wet April.

Sophia began to worry about the state of the trail. Three people had been killed in floods just that month. The city had taken to implementing its own flood warnings in addition to those from the National Weather Service. The local warnings made it illegal to drive downtown at all when the waters got to a certain level. Flash floods really scared Sophia because they were sneaky. People couldn't tell from other parts of the city that downtown was completely submerged, so they would set out for a dinner date or to see a play and get caught up in the flood. The first two people to be killed had been like that. The man was in a tuxedo and the woman was wearing a pastel green evening gown. They had been on their way to a charity ball to raise money for the Nelson-Atkins Museum of Art. Now the museum was raising money for their orphaned six-year-old son.

Sophia checked the forecast in the newspaper to be sure it matched the one on the radio. "Mostly cloudy and breezy," it assured her. *Hopefully we won't run into any high water coming from somewhere upriver*, Sophia thought, as she closed the paper.

As soon as they prayed the dawn prayer, Sophia's dad was ready to get on the road. Sophia started the car for him. Of course, in May it didn't really *need* to be started ahead of time, but Sophia enjoyed doing it.

She could have applied for her permit a year earlier, but her parents had made her wait until she turned 16. "Insurance is too high," they'd said. Amani had already been driving for four months, and Sophia was older than she was! But she had only a month left to go and she was trying to get all the driving experience she could. Sophia was surprised at the fact that she wasn't the least bit afraid when she thought about driving. Amani had been scared at first. She had driven for weeks in an empty parking lot and then on a cemetery road before she'd had the guts to go into the street. Maybe it was because she'd had to wait so long, or maybe it was because when she was behind the wheel she felt in control of things, but Sophia was confident she'd be able to drive without any problems. She couldn't wait.

Back inside, Sophia looped her long braid in half and secured it with a band. She was famous among her friends for her long, thick, dark brown hair. She had never had it cut until last year, when it was down to her knees and became so heavy she was getting headaches. Then she'd finally given in and had it cut to just below her waist. She'd donated the 23 inches to Locks of Love to make wigs for chemo patients. She grabbed her backpack, added some extra seed and some grapes to Kuzko's dishes, kissed him goodbye, and headed out. As she was stepping out the door, her mom called from upstairs.

"Sophi! Do you have a safety pin I can use?" In a house with Muslim women who have to pin their scarves, safety pins disappear faster than sock mates. Sophia and her mother bought them in plastic boxes of 100 each, but somehow the pin dish they kept in the upstairs hall was always empty. Sophia headed back to her room and grabbed a pin from her emergency stash. As an afterthought, she took a few more and threw them into her backpack. Then she saw her phone lying on the bed and was glad she'd remembered to charge it the night before. She grabbed it and, looping up the charger, stuck them both in the outside pocket of her backpack, along with her pencils.

DeSoto was only about 30 miles from their home in Leawood, a suburb of Kansas City. Sophia, resident bookworm, always kept a book tucked under the back seat, so she was good to go. Hisham spent the entire trip absorbed in *Mario* and *Star Wars* on his Gameboy, and their mom had just finished her spring finals at the University of Missouri, where she was studying to be a physician's assistant, so the usual book in *her* hands was replaced by a crochet hook.

Sophia dozed and when she opened her eyes they were pulling onto the dirt road that would take them to the bike trail. There was a beautiful old farmhouse right on the corner, with a wraparound porch and a large stand of trees in the back. The house was white with green shutters. A beautifully refurbished red barn stood behind it. A sign out front read, "Underground Railroad Station." Sophia made a note of it so she could suggest it as a field trip for Sr. Iman's history class next year.

"It's a good thing I didn't wash the car yesterday like I was going to!" exclaimed her dad as they bumped over the still-muddy washboard road.

"I hope the trail is drier than this," fretted Sophia.

"I hope it's wetter!" said Hisham, sitting up a bit in his seat. "I want to splash through puddles just like on the Mountain Dew commercial. 'Do the Dew!'" he quoted.

"Sorry, Hisham. The trail itself is paved."

"Thank God!" Sophia's mom whispered to her without letting her dad hear.

Sophia rolled down her window. The air was damp and soft and smelled of fresh-cut grass. She took a deep breath and began to really look forward to the bike ride.

The river that ran along the right side of the bike path was swollen so much it had engulfed its sandbars, the small islands of sand that usually sat in the middle of it. Small trees poked up out of the water, and Sophia saw debris on the bike path that told her the river had been up high enough at one point to flow over the spot they were riding on. Sophia had never seen the water move so swiftly. The usually meandering Kansas River looked robust and vigorous—like rivers you see in movies. The path was dry, though, and it *looked* far enough away from the sloping banks to be safe. Sophia imagined her bike skidding into the river and blinked the thought away. The family did a bit of a warm-up stretch and then started off toward the west, along the riverbank. Sophia's backpack was a bit heavy and she almost wished she hadn't brought so much stuff—or at least that she could trade backpacks with Hisham!

By the time they had been biking for about an hour and a half, the sun was well up behind the clouds and Sophia needed a break. The wind had picked up a little bit and was working against them. That was nice as it kept them cool—it was probably about 80 degrees already and they were all sweating—but it made the pedaling tougher. They had also been biking slightly uphill the whole time. Sophia was glad it was cloudy; at least the sun wasn't bearing down on them. Her dad was out in front and didn't seem as winded as Sophia was. Hisham was in front of Sophia, and he had been whining for a break for half an hour already. Her mom was bringing up the rear—not because she was a wimp but because she had stopped to pick flowers. She was also beginning to sneeze and sniffle.

"Dad, can we please stop? I'm staaaaarrrving," Hisham begged again. He was in really good shape from playing basketball in the winter and running track in the spring, but he had to eat about every thirty seconds or he would have a conniption. Sophia had never seen anyone get mad when they were hungry, but Hisham did. Even his friends knew that if he was cranky, they should try feeding him.

Sophia's dad stopped his bike, turned around and waited for the rest of the family to catch up.

"Alright, there's a bend right at the top of this slope, see it? Overlooking that bank? We'll stop there and eat breakfast."

Sophia knew that "breakfast" consisted of the protein bars and orange juice her dad had put in his backpack. He was planning on getting to Lawrence in time to eat a late lunch there. Sophia hoped there was enough protein in the bars to keep Hisham happy that whole time.

When they arrived at the spot her dad had indicated, Hisham headed straight to the edge of the bank to check out the river. Sophia dropped her backpack onto the ground and stretched out her shoulders. It felt great to lighten her load. She wondered if you could give yourself scoliosis by riding with a heavy backpack.

Sophia edged slowly up to the spot where Hisham was throwing rocks into the river. Then she stepped abruptly back as a wave of vertigo hit her from glancing down into the rushing water. The gently sloping sandbars they had seen earlier had given way to steep, sandy drop-offs, and there was a distance of about fifteen feet between her and the water. But that wasn't the scariest thing. The scariest thing was the river itself. The passage below them was narrow—a lot narrower than the river had been where they'd started out—and the river was rushing along, fighting and tripping over itself to squeeze through the constricted gorge, carrying sticks and muck along the top of it.

Upstream a bit to their left was a small waterfall, about five or six feet tall. As the water reached the bottom it churned and stirred itself for a few more feet and then smoothed out a bit to slide along a bit less violently, but still pretty choppy. Right underneath them, though, it went through a patch of jagged backflows and yellow-white rapids just like the ones Sophia had seen people kayaking through on The Discovery Channel. The roar was so loud they almost didn't hear their dad when he came up to join them.

"That's Devil's Drop-off," he told them casually, while Sophia sat down to avoid the feeling that she was about to topple over into the water. "Your mother and I used to come out here and sit on the rocks in the middle of the river when we were first married. When the river is down real low you can see the place where the bottom of the riverbed juts out and then just drops off. And there's a big rock right about there," he pointed toward a particularly wild vortex of water that was sucking some branches into its grip. "It's flat on top and big enough to picnic on. Bring the phone, hon'!" he called to Sophia's mom.

"*SubhanAllah*!" she breathed when she reached them. "I've never seen it like this!" Sophia's dad took the phone from her and started snapping pictures.

When he had gotten the river from every possible angle, they went back and sat on a log that was lying near the path. Sophia's dad broke out the protein bars and gave one each to her and her mom. Then he gave three to Hisham. The orange juice he gave them was in plastic bottles, but Sophia was sure it would only make her thirstier. She asked her mom if she'd brought any water.

"Yeah, in that little carrying case under my bike seat." she answered. "Did you bring any Benadryl?" Sophia's mom suffered from killer allergies, but she always relied on Sophia to bring her medicine, since she usually carried a first aid kit *and* a virtual pharmacy with her.

Sophia opened the box of Benadryl and gave a caplet to her mom. Then she tucked the box back into her backpack and gratefully chugged the cool, crisp water.

As Sophia sat on the log and ate her protein bar, she watched a small chipmunk near a tree. He seemed to be waiting for something, so Sophia tossed him a crumb. He came right up and ate it, and Sophia realized the trail must usually be pretty busy. This chipmunk was used to people. It had been pretty deserted this morning, though. They'd only passed one other family on bikes and a couple walking hand-in-hand, going the other way. Too damp to camp, Sophia guessed.

She threw the chipmunk another crumb, about a foot closer to her. When he finished the first one, he came for the second. Sophia sat stock-still and watched him eat the crumb just like a sandwich in his little hands. She didn't want him to get too close, because she knew that wild animals carried things like fleas and lice and even rabies, so she threw him the last corner of her bar and watched him eat it about a foot away from her toes. He sniffed around and waited a few more minutes, hoping for more, but when Sophia's dad came over and announced it was time to get going, he scampered away.

"Maybe we can make it all the way to Lawrence before the sun breaks through this cloud cover," her dad said, as he hopped on his bike.

Sophia stood up and picked up her backpack. As she heaved it onto her shoulders, the crinkly metallic wrapper from her protein bar fell out of her hand. A small gust of wind plucked it from the air and blew it across the bike path. Sophia caught up to it about two feet from the edge of the drop off; it had caught near the ground in the branches of a bush growing by the side of the bank. Its leaves caught her eye as she stooped to pick up the wrapper—they were dark green on top and a pale, almost translucent green underneath.

She wasn't even running anymore, but when she bent down, the weight of her backpack caused her to stumble forward a step. In that instant, the sandy ground beneath her feet gave way. Sophia, fighting to keep her balance, backpedaled on the tumbling ground with her arms flailing wildly. She tried to grab the branches of the bush, but they slipped through her hand. She heard her mom scream her name and felt herself somersault before she hit the freezing, violent water.

Sophia was shocked by the temperature of the water more than anything else. She was so shocked that for a split second she did nothing—just adjusted to the sudden temperature change. Then she realized she was underwater and didn't even know which way the surface was—and her backpack was dragging at her. Her body went on automatic pilot and she shot her legs out straight in an attempt to touch the bottom of the river—or at least determine which way it was. Nothing.

Sophia spread her arms and began to push against the water. Eventually her head broke the surface—although whether it was from her efforts or just dumb luck she couldn't tell—and she took a huge gulp of air. Her scarf tail was in front of her face and she pushed it away, opening her eyes.

The entire world was a blur of dark, muddy water and white, churning foam. "Help me, *ya Allah!*" Sophia thought briefly, and then her head struck the picnic rock and she saw nothing.

Sophia blacked out for only a second. When she came to, she was being dragged back under by the current and her heavy backpack. She managed to keep her head above water, taking short, gulping breaths and holding them in case she was churned under again. She was struggling to take her backpack off when she saw a fallen tree that was perched across the river at an odd angle. The current tore at her clothes trying to pull her away from her one chance at safety. Sophia said, "*Bismillah*," and kicked her way toward the tree trunk. If she could just get close enough to catch a branch as she was swept by.

The moment came. She grabbed for the tree. Her hand slid on the branch she had managed to clasp, scraping her skin, but she didn't even notice. She held on to the branch and was able to catch it with her other hand. She rested there for a few seconds, while the water tried to bully her back into its grasp, and then she began pulling herself along the tree toward the shore, grasping branch after branch like crossing monkey bars. Even though the trip was only about ten feet, it seemed to take forever. At last she reached the shore. The bank was just a gentle slope this far downstream, and Sophia was able to climb completely free of the water. She shrugged off her backpack, sat against the trunk of the fallen tree, and closed her eyes.

"*Ya Latif*," she sputtered. Then she coughed several times and choked up a good bit of water. She picked a small piece of a twig out of her mouth and relaxed, waiting for her parents and Hisham to come. After catching her breath, she began to survey the damage.

Her scarf was ripped at the bottom and of course it was filthy. Her long shirt was kind of a tangled mess, bunched up around her waist, but there were no tears that she could see in it, and her jeans didn't seem to be any the worse for wear at all. Her new sneakers were gone. She didn't even remember them coming off. She was soaked to the bone, her backpack was soggy, her hand was scraped up, but at least she wasn't hurt in any serious way. Then she remembered her head. . .

Sophia took off her scarf and reached up, feeling the place on the right side of her head where she had been personally introduced to the picnic rock—for she was sure it had been that large rock her dad had told her about that she'd hit. It was painful and starting to swell, but there was no blood. That was a bad sign. Sophia began to worry. If her head was not bleeding *outside*, that didn't mean it wasn't bleeding *inside*. She knew she had blacked out momentarily; that meant she might have a serious concussion or significant internal bleeding! A head injury like that could paralyze a person—or worse!

Sophia felt her head again. She was sure it had swollen even more in the brief seconds she'd been inspecting herself. She started to panic. If she had a head injury, time was of the essence. And she had no idea where she was in relation to the car. She looked down, caught sight of her backpack, and remembered that her phone was in its outer pocket. It was probably ruined. She unzipped the pocket and found the phone a bit wet but still working. She opened it and a small square blinked out at her. "Looking for Service" it said. "I should have known," moaned Sophia. She laid it next to her backpack to dry and stood up.

Swooning a bit, she looked behind her and upstream. No one was coming. She began to get nauseous. *Oh, great*, she thought. *The first sign of a concussion!*

It was then that Sophia realized she was trembling. Surely her parents should be coming along soon—it wouldn't take them long to ride their bikes back down the slope to her. Sophia called for her mom but the effort hurt her head. Her panic was growing and she was certain she was going to throw up. She sat back down.

Ya Allah, help me, she thought. And then she began reciting the *tasbih dhikr*. "*SubhanAllah wa Alhamdulillah wa La illaha il Allah wa Allahu Akbar*. . .All glory to God, and All thanks to God, there is no God but God, and God is the Greatest."

It helped, and she managed to keep the protein bar in her stomach. After a few minutes, the wave of nausea passed. She listened for sirens or maybe even a helicopter, because she was sure her parents would have called 911, especially since they hadn't found her right away. She hoped they had biked close enough to Lawrence to have entered a coverage area for her dad's phone.

But what if she'd been washed farther downriver than she thought. . .Maybe she had blacked out for a longer period of time than she imagined?

This idea struck Sophia like lightening bolt. What if she'd been washed far downriver and it would take a long time for the searchers to find her? What if the reason she didn't see the bike path was because she'd passed the point where it began? Sophia choked back tears and put her head on her knees. She suddenly realized she was shivering as much from cold as from fear; her wet clothes were clinging to her and her fingernails were blue.

"Thank God it's sunny," she said out loud, and as she said it, she remembered that it had still been completely overcast when she and her family had stopped for breakfast.

SOPHIA LOOKED UP. THE sun was indeed shining. There were clouds in the sky but not the heavy, solid clouds of earlier that morning. These were puffier and broken up. In fact, there was as much clear sky as there were clouds. And the sun was almost directly overhead.

Ya Rabbi! Sophia thought. *What time is it? How long was I unconscious?*

She listened intently. The sound of the river rushing by was unbroken, although it wasn't rushing as fast here as it had been upstream because the riverbed was wider. She listened for several seconds; she heard birds and insects from behind her but no sirens or choppers.

Sophia wondered if she should look in her backpack and see if her other clothes had gotten wet. Maybe if she was lucky they would be dry since the backpack was leather. Leather was waterproof, wasn't it? Cows' insides didn't get wet. When she found herself thinking about cows' insides she decided she needed to do something to keep busy. Even though she held out little hope that her things were dry, going through her backpack would keep her occupied until the rescue people or her parents arrived.

First things first, though. Sophia needed to get her hand bandaged up. Now that the adrenaline was gone it was really beginning to throb. The scrapes were deeper than she'd thought at first. Sophia ventured back to the river's edge. She didn't want to get near the water again, but she had to wash out those cuts so they didn't get infected.

She squatted down about a foot from the water and stuck her hand out. She knew the water was far from sanitary but it was the only water around, so she went ahead and sloshed her hand around for several seconds in the river. When she withdrew it, it looked a bit cleaner, so she headed back up the slope to dress it with antibiotic ointment and bandages. Then Sophia sank to the ground in her sunny spot and opened her backpack.

She started with the main compartment. The only water that had gotten in had come from around the zipper at the top.

"Wow! Cow's insides really do stay dry," she said aloud, and smiled for the first time since she'd tumbled into the river. The nausea hadn't come back again and Sophia didn't feel inordinately sleepy, so she allowed herself to think that maybe she didn't have a concussion after all. Her fingers shook from cold and she prayed her clothes would be dry enough to wear. Each little breeze that came along went straight to her bones. The same breezes that she'd been thankful for earlier that day!

The worst casualties of the accident were the new pink flats she'd packed to wear with her skirt, which were at the very top. They were soaked and the padding was already coming off from the soles. Her first aid kit was next. She'd regretted bringing it earlier because of the extra weight it had added to her backpack, but she sure was glad for her caution now. The kit and the prayer rug underneath it were pretty wet. She looked inside the first aid kit and was relieved to find that the itch cream, antibiotic ointment, Tylenol, bandages, gauze, alcohol wipes, and tape inside were safe and dry. Even her mom's Benadryl was still dry, as it was packed in individual foil-wrapped packages.

Thankfully, the most important item in the kit, her Epi-pen, was also undamaged. After her bout with the bee as a child, she'd had allergy tests that showed she was allergic to bees and shellfish. Shellfish were usually pretty easy to avoid—especially in Kansas—but bees did not always understand the avoidance concept. So whenever she was going to be outdoors she had to carry the pen, which was actually a small syringe filled with epinephrine, to stick herself with in case of a sting.

The doctor said another sting like the one when she was small might result in anaphylactic shock—and even death—before she would be able to get to the hospital. The pen was her lifeline.

Sophia took out a bandage and the antibiotic ointment and dressed her palm. Then she took the prayer rug out and found the beige peasant skirt and blouse she'd packed in case her family went out to eat with their cousins. Her pink and beige flower print scarf was folded neatly inside the skirt. The extra clothes were a bit damp, but certainly more dry than what she had on! Sophia left her backpack where it was and picked her way carefully up to the trees. There was undergrowth and shrubbery everywhere. She ducked behind a large bush to change, being careful not to touch any leaves because she wasn't *exactly* sure what poison ivy looked like. She considered leaving her feet bare since she didn't have any shoes anyway, but went ahead and put on her clean socks because her feet were so cold, and at least they afforded some protection from the rocks and twigs.

Once out of her wet clothes and into her mostly dry skirt, top and scarf, Sophia immediately felt warmer. Back at her backpack, she spread her wet clothes and prayer rug out on the ground to dry. Bending over to do so made her head throb and she felt her sore spot again. It was the size of a small egg. Sophia wished she could at least put some ice on it. She improvised with one of her wet socks, and sat down carefully to finish going through her things.

At the very bottom of her backpack she found the small photo album she had packed to show her cousin. Still dry, *alhamdulillah*. It held the pictures that Sophia and Amani had taken during the last month of school. Sophia's cousin, Tasneem, had lived in Leawood before her dad had gotten a job in Lawrence, and she really missed the girls at Sophia's school. Sophia had brought the album to share with her. She flipped through it quickly and set it aside.

The compass, pens, and toiletries in the outside pocket had all gotten wet but wouldn't suffer any permanent damage. She set them aside with her photo album and then opened her backpack to the sun. Once that was done, though, she didn't know what else to do.

Sophia estimated that at least twenty minutes had gone by since she had crawled out of the river. She was working hard to swallow the terror that threatened to rise up from her chest. What if her parents didn't find her? She wondered how weak her immune system would get from being so cold and wet. She could come down with pneumonia! Or her hand could become infected and she could lose it to gangrene! A small spider crawled across her prayer rug, and this presented Sophia with a new worry: spiders and snakes! And leeches! She had been in the water for she didn't know how long. . . Sophia began to check her scalp and skin for hitchhikers. When she didn't find any, she calmed down a little.

The moment of terror passed, and she realized she needed to take some steps to find out what her situation was and how she might be able to get out of it herself if help didn't come in time. She decided to venture through the bushes and past the small stand of trees behind them that lined the bank. This was not as easy as she'd expected it to be. Between her throbbing head and her tender socked feet she had to pick her way slowly through the trees. She was rewarded for all this effort by a huge expanse of tall, wavy, light green grass that began just beyond the trees. *Must be some kind of hay field*, she thought. *I must really have been swept past the bike trail.*

Sophia trekked back through the trees and sat back down by her backpack. Looking at the racing water, she waited. The river rushed by but didn't offer her any answers in its hurry. She decided that when her things dried a bit she would set out upstream, back toward where she assumed the bike trail began. She'd walk slowly and carefully along the bank, so as not to aggravate her head injury or step on any dangerous plants. Or broken bottles! Or worse!

With a start, Sophia remembered an email she had received once that warned of used syringes left by junkies in the least suspected places, like

Playland ball pits and sandboxes. She expected there was probably tons of stuff like that buried just beneath the surface of the grass and sand. How had she walked all the way through the trees with no shoes on? She felt her pink flats but they were still pretty wet. No matter, though. She would wear them wet rather than walk upriver without them!

Sophia checked her clothes. Her t-shirt was starting to dry out but her jeans were still completely soaked. She looked at the sun and found it beginning to descend. She decided that if no one had come to rescue her by the time of the afternoon prayer, about four in the afternoon, when shadows were the same size as their objects, she would start walking. In the meantime, she just had to sit still and not panic.

Sitting still made her realize she was starving. It was a sudden, urgent hunger, because up until then she had been preoccupied and hadn't realized she was hungry at all. "I wish I hadn't fed half my protein bar to that chipmunk," she said to herself.

The sound of the river and the warmth of the sun began to lull Sophia into sleepiness. She leaned back on the slope, slid her prayer rug out from underneath her toiletries, and rolled it up for a pillow. Then she eased herself down onto it. She fought sleep because she knew that people with possible concussions should not be allowed to drop off, and because she didn't want to become spider bait, but the trauma of the day had just been too much for her and the sun was so comforting. . .she drifted off to sleep and stopped worrying for a couple of hours.

WHEN SOPHIA WOKE, THE shadows were long. She realized she'd slept past noon prayer and the afternoon prayer had long been in. After taking a few minutes to wake up, get her bearings, and feel her head again, she made her ablution in the river, washing her hands awkwardly around her bandage, then her arms, face, and feet. Sophia prayed the noon and afternoon prayers together, shortening them since she was traveling.

After she finished praying, she decided to go ahead and start walking. Her things were drier now, although her jeans and backpack were still pretty damp. That was OK, though; she would have to wash them all when she got home, anyway. She rolled the damp jeans up and wrapped them in the prayer rug. She put her toiletries into the outer pocket of the backpack along with her mom's cell phone, laid the first aid kit, photo album, and medicines in the bottom of her pack where it was driest, and tucked her other t-shirt in last. She zipped the zippers and stood up, bringing the backpack up with her, and settling it on her shoulders. When she turned to slip her feet into her damp pink shoes, she almost fell back down from shock. She was greeted by the sight of an old farmer and an equally old horse at the top of the slope. She'd been so absorbed in packing her bag, and the river was so loud, that she hadn't heard them approach.

"Afternoon, Miss," he greeted her, lifting the woven straw hat he wore. "Name's Jacques Bodine. Sorry to give yeh such a start. We'as on our way into Westport and stopped by fer a drink."

"Uhhh. . .afternoon," Sophia answered, getting her voice back and looking around to make sure he was talking to her, even though she knew she was alone. "I'm Sophia Ahmed." She was as surprised by the man's looks as she was by his presence. He had a long white beard and what appeared to be canvas or burlap overalls. His dirty white shirt had a rounded collar and he had a pack of some kind on his back. He was holding his horse by a rope. Sophia had only seen horses up close a couple of times before. She was startled at how big it was— its shoulders were almost level with the farmer's head.

"You OK? You look a bit befuddled. . .you need some hep?"

Sophia looked down at her feet. Embarrassed, she slipped her feet into her flats and tugged her skirt down.

"Um, yes, please. I fell in the river and was washed downstream. I'm looking for the bike trail. My parents are probably going crazy by now."

"The bike trail?"

"Yes. The one that goes into Lawrence."

"Well, the Oregon goes through Lawrence. The Santa Fe goes south o' there. I ain't never heard tell a' no 'Bike Trail' afore. But I'm on my way into Westport with these here furs. I kin take yeh ta Maddy Collins' place. Yeh kin figger it out from there." Sophia hadn't noticed the pile of furs strapped to his horse's back. The man adjusted his. . .business. . .and spat on the ground. Sophia tried not to shudder.

"Uhhh. . ." she began uncertainly, wary of the stranger who was obviously a bit off his rocker, but at the same time realizing she didn't have too many other choices. Her upbringing told her not to go with the strange man, but he was old and probably out of shape. If it came down to it, she was sure she could outrun him. She finally decided to let him lead her to the lady's house. Then she could call her parents. "Uh, yeah. I'd appreciate that. I could use the phone from there. Thank you, Mr. Bodine."

Jacques Bodine cast her a sidelong glance, as though he found her very peculiar. He must think she was crazy, or that she had hit her head ever harder than she had.

Sophia was wondering similar things about him. He sure seemed strange.

As she joined Mr. Bodine and they emerged at the top of the rise, she began to wish she hadn't agreed to go with him. He smelled like Hisham's locker the time he left his gym socks in there over the weekend. And the furs smelled, too. A musky, "dead things" kind of smell.

"How far is it?" she asked, as they began to walk through the grass.

"Oh, 'bout a quarter mile. This here's the Collins land," he indicated the general area they were walking through and then looked at Sophia, concerned. "Kin yeh walk it?"

"Oh, yeah. Yeah, I can walk. I'm OK." They had entered a trail leading through the tall grass off to their right, but that was the only sign of civilization. She was really in the middle of nowhere—and there was no bike trail in sight. As far as she could see, in all directions except the way they'd come, there were tiny rolling hills with tall grass glowing in the sun and waving in the breeze. They stayed on the path and, as they came to the top of a small ridge, Sophia could see the Collins place.

Mr. Bodine chattered about his horse, Emily, and how old she was getting. Sophia didn't really listen or respond. She was thinking of other things. Like how to get away if this guy wanted to add her skin to his pelt collection.

5

IT TOOK SOPHIA AND Mr. Bodine about twenty minutes to reach the Collins place. During that time, the sun set. Although the sky turned azure and then gray around her, and the sun was enormous and majestically orange as it dipped below the prairie, Sophia could not appreciate the beauty of it. She had really started to panic. Not so much for herself as for her parents. They were out there somewhere looking for her, probably frantic. It was getting dark, and she had no way of letting them know she was safe.

The house she'd seen from the ridge wasn't exactly a house. It was a cabin. A small, one-room affair, with what looked like a shed about 20 yards to the side. Someone was chopping wood behind the cabin and Mr. Bodine led Sophia around back.

"Maddy!" Mr. Bodine called as they approached, and to Sophia's surprise a young man about 20 years old looked up. He was on the other side of the woodpile and didn't see her right away. Sophia blinked. Mr. Bodine must have been saying "Matty" instead of "Maddy."

"Jacques! You old coot, you!" came the friendly answer as the young man doffed his felt hat and wiped his brow. When he emerged from behind the woodpile and saw Sophia, it was his turn to be shocked. He stopped in his tracks and just looked from her to Mr. Bodine and back.

"Matty, this here's Miss Sophia." He gestured toward her. "And this is Matthew Collins. Miss Sophia took a tumble inta th' Kansas and needs to get back to the 'Bike Trail' and find her folks. You ever heard tell of a 'Bike Trail' round these parts?"

Matthew Collins looked at her with genuine concern. "Well, I've heard people call the Oregon the Bison Trail. Maybe it's short for that?" He looked at Sophia, as if expecting her to provide the answer.

She tried. "No, it's the bike trail. By the river. It goes from DeSoto to Lawrence. We were riding this morning—we were supposed to spend the night with my cousins in Lawrence—and I fell down a steep bank and got washed downstream. . ."

"She got knocked in the head," Mr. Bodine said meaningfully, tilting his head toward Sophia and raising his eyebrows.

"Listen, if I could just use your. . ." and that's when the import of Matthew Collins' clothes dawned on Sophia. He was wearing pants held up by suspenders, no shoes, and a faded cotton shirt. *He's Amish!* she realized. *He probably doesn't even have electricity.*

"I. . .don't suppose you have a phone?" she asked him.

"Ummm. . .not so's you'd notice," he answered, gesturing helplessly to his simple home and cocking his head questioningly toward Mr. Bodine. "But why don't you come on in. Does your head hurt? I can give you something for it and then hitch up the wagon and take you to the Sampson place. Maybe they know about the trail you're lookin' for. It's too late to set out tonight, but we can search for your folks in the morning. I'd welcome you to stay here, but it wouldn't be seemly. I live here alone."

As he spoke, he guided Sophia into the house and sat her at a small table that was really a large trunk with wooden benches on either side. The only light came from a kerosene lantern on the top of the trunk. It smelled strong but homey.

Matthew ducked into a cupboard, which consisted of a small curtain pulled in front of some shelves, produced a glass medicine bottle, and poured some of it into a tin cup. "Here. This'll help your head." He handed her the cup.

Sophia sniffed it. It smelled like strong, nasty cough syrup.

And she didn't even know this guy! What if it was poison or had illegal drugs in it? There was no way she could drink it. She started to object.

"I know it tastes somethin' awful, but it's just the thing for pain," he reassured her. "My sister made me bring it with me and am I glad she did! I used it when I had the ague right after I got out here last winter." Whatever "ague" was.

Sophia weighed her options. Glancing around at the young man's simple cabin, she was sure he wasn't a drug pusher or a criminal. The house was neat and he actually had some kind of horse harness lying across the chair by the fireplace, with a sewing needle sticking out of it. He couldn't possibly be evil. And her head did hurt.

"*Bismillah*," she prayed silently, "In the name of God," and downed the quarter cup of liquid in one swallow. It was bitter and oily. Sophia found herself gagging. Was that castor oil? Matthew handed her a ladle with some water in it. She thanked him and gulped the water while he rejoined Mr. Bodine outside.

"So you'll take 'er to the Sampson place tonight?" she heard Jacques ask.

"Yeah. I'll hitch up the wagon and take her now. Good thing you found her, Jacques. I think she took quite a knock on the head. An immigrant like her would've had a hard time out there by the river all alone."

Sophia thought that was an awfully ignorant thing to assume just because she wore a scarf. *I'm just as American as they are*, she thought to herself indignantly. But then she remembered they were Amish and didn't have TV or even radios. They had probably never seen a Muslim before.

"I'll camp by the river tonight and ride over there in the morning. Maybe Joseph and I can go into Westport together tomorrow and ask around about her," she heard Mr. Bodine say.

"You sure you don't want to bunk with me tonight?" Matthew offered.

"Nah. I do better outdoors."

Sophia got up and met Matthew outside. He motioned for her to climb aboard and started to help her into the back, but she was already up the ladder that led to the back of the wagon. This wasn't the small black carriage-type of wagon Sophia always saw Amish people riding in when she and her family passed the Amish community of Yoder on the way to visit her grandparents. This was a work wagon. A simple wooden box on big wooden wheels. The floor was covered with straw and she sat down in it while Matthew climbed up onto the board seat and clucked to the horses.

Sophia leaned back on the side of the wagonbed and looked at the stars. The night was completely dark and there were more stars than she had ever seen. Bright and clear and brilliant. "*SubhanAllah,*" Sophia breathed. She found the Big Dipper, although it was harder than usual because there were more stars surrounding it than when she looked up at night from her house in Leawood, where the bright lights of Kansas City drowned out all but the most determined twinkles.

Just as Sophia began to wonder how far it was to the Sampson place, the stars began to blur together and she got very drowsy. *That medicine is making me sleepy*, she thought, but fought again to stay awake so she could explain her situation to the Sampsons. She checked the cell phone one more time. Still no signal, and now the battery was a 12%. She began reciting the *tasbih* again and soon, despite her best efforts, the rocking of the wagon lulled her to sleep. Just before dropping off she prayed that the medicine she'd taken wasn't poison after all.

SOPHIA DIDN'T KNOW WHAT time it was; it felt like she had slept forever. There was only dim light in the room, and she couldn't tell if it was early morning or late evening. She had a hard time keeping her eyes open, because they were scratchy and stung, so she lay for a while, opening them only briefly and blinking the sting away. The pain in her head reminded her what had happened, but she still didn't recognize the room she was in. Had she slept through another whole day? Surely not! The thought panicked her. What if she had, and her parents were still out there, wondering where she was? Then she remembered that Jacques and Matthew had brought her to someone else's house, and she was suddenly embarrassed. She hated the idea of imposing on complete strangers like this. Her cut hand was wrapped in soft cloth and she was comfortably tucked in a bed, so these people had obviously taken care of her. And she hadn't even seen them! Now she had to meet them and thank them and somehow repay them. How humiliating.

"The water's on the table, Ma!" she heard a young girl say, and then heard the clunk of a pitcher or bucket on a wooden table.

"Thank you, Abby," she heard from outside.

Sophia tried to sit up, but when she did her head spun. She laid back, closed her eyes again, and waited for the room to calm down. Soon she tried opening her eyes again. She fluttered her eye lids until they were at least able to stay open, and then tried to focus on the room around her. The floor was dirt. Even Amish people didn't have dirt floors, did they?

Weak sunlight streamed in from the only window in the room, near the bed where Sophia found herself, and the open door let in the only other light. A large, black, cast-iron stove presided over the far end of the room. A table with small stools and a rocking chair by the bed were the only other furniture. The wall near Sophia's head was covered with a sort of ivory-colored wallpaper, that, when Sophia's blurry vision cleared, she realized was actually newspaper. Whoa. Sophia knew that the Amish were simple people, but this house seemed a *lot* simpler than the cheery wooden farmhouses she'd seen in Yoder.

"Ma?" called the girl again. "Will Mr. Bodine be

comin' home with Pa tonight?"

"I don't know, honey. Depends on whether or not they find Miss Sophia's train, I expect. I wouldn't be surprised if they came back early, if they find it. Her family is probably worried sick."

Sophia's eyes snapped wide open at the word "train." Abby and her mom were talking outside and she could no longer make out their words. But then she wasn't really listening anymore. Why did they think she had been on a train? Maybe when Mr. Bodine told them "bike trail" they had thought he said, "bike train?" The confusion made her head throb and she needed a minute to get her thoughts together. She turned over toward the wall so they wouldn't see she was awake if they happened to come in again.

As she stared at the newspaper, a picture slowly came into focus. It was a drawing of a woman wearing a hoop skirt. It advertised the most comfortable fitting steel hoops in the territory. Sophia read the headline next to it.

Henry Adams Attends
President Buchanan's Inauguration

And another:

Local Woman Attends National Rally
for Women's Suffrage

Sophia blinked again. The panic was coming

back. She scoured desperately for the date of the newspaper. The top of the page was covered by the bottom of the page above it. Sophia had to search for a page with the date on it. She found one in the row above.

"January, 1857," it read.

January, 1857? Who decorates their bedroom wall with imitation newsprint from 150 years ago? *Oh, my God!* Sophia thought suddenly. What if she really was in 1857? Surely not, she chided herself.

She forced herself to calm down. Breathing in slowly through her nose, she exhaled and whispered, "*La hawla wa la quwwata illa bi lah,*" There is no power or authority except with God. She cleared her mind as much as possible so she could think. Maybe this was one of those living history setups? Sr. Iman had shown her class a video last year about people in Pennsylvania who lived in a colonial reenactment community. They lived for three months at a time in a colonial-era community. Tourists would visit and watch them go about their daily lives. They had kids and pets and everything, and the kids even went to school there during the school year. That's probably what this was. A pioneer reenactment community. Surely they had a phone *somewhere*.

A spark of anger started to grow in Sophia's chest. How dare these people not try to find her parents! Couldn't they break their precious act for an obvious emergency?

Sophia turned over and slowly dragged her legs off the bed. She was sore and stiff, and had to sit for minute before she could even think about standing. Her hand stung and her throat ached from thirst, but her anger spurred her on. She knew she probably looked like the *Creature from the Black Lagoon*, but she didn't care. She started to stand. She had to go to the bathroom.

Just then Abby came back into the house and Sophia saw her for the first time. She was a slight young girl, about fourteen years old, with sun-streaked blonde hair braided into a long rope that hung down her back. She wore a simple brown, frock-like dress, no shoes, and a sunbonnet around her neck. When she saw Sophia awake, her face went suddenly shy.

"Good morning," she said quietly.

"Oh! Is Miss Sophia up?" Abby's mother came into the house, drying her hands on her apron. She was followed by a large yellow dog, attached to a friendly, wagging tail. "Sadie, stay," she commanded. And then to Sophia, "Oh, sit back down, dear. Don't try to move. You've had quite a time. Let me have a look at you. How do you feel?"

Sophia tried to answer but her voice was shaky and gravelly, and her throat hurt. She sort of croaked. She wound up just nodding with a weak smile, and sank back gratefully onto the bed as another wave of dizziness washed over her. She was even weaker than she'd thought.

Sophia's anger faded as she took in the figure before her. The kind woman who looked down on her was younger than she'd expected. Her brown hair, which was wrapped into a knot at the nape of her neck, was sort of mousy, but her face was broad and smiling. She was open and caring, and Sophia wondered if she was a nurse back in the "real world."

"Abby, get Miss Sophia the dipper, and fetch me the rag." She felt Sophia's forehead and started to unwrap her hand. "We were hoping you'd get a good night's rest. You were so exhausted last night that you didn't even wake up when Joseph and Mr. Bodine carried you in here."

Abby had brought the dipper, and her mother offered it to Sophia. She sipped the cool water slowly, because even drinking water hurt her throat, it was so dry and swollen. She realized as she drank that she'd had almost no water at all since yesterday at the clearing when her family had stopped for breakfast. The thought of her family brought her back to reality.

As she handed the dipper back with a smile of gratitude, she asked, "Do you have a phone? I need to call my family."

Abby and her mother looked at each other. Finally her mother said, "My husband, Joseph, went with Jacques Bodine into Westport this morning to look for your family. Do you think you can answer a few questions? I need to know where you fell into the river."

Sophia tested her voice again. It wasn't normal, but it was at least working. "I don't know. It was between here and Lawrence. The river was narrow there, and the banks were very steep. I hit my head on a big, flat rock in the middle of the river." As she said that Sophia began to wonder if that was the explanation for all this. Maybe her head injury was causing her to hallucinate. Was that possible?

"Did you injure your insides anywhere?" asked Abby's mother.

"No. Just my hand and my head."

"That's good to know. Well, I'm Eleanor Sampson, and this is my daughter Abigail." By then a boy of about ten had joined Sadie in the doorway, obviously curious about the visitor.

"And that is Joshua." Joshua's face erupted in a friendly smile that matched his mother's. He had darker hair than Abby, and his face was sprinkled with boyish freckles.

"I'm Sophia Ahmed. Thank you so much for taking care of me. I'm sorry to have put you to so much trouble."

"Oh, don't be silly! No trouble at all. We're glad to help out. Now, there's a basin on the table if you'd like to wash up. You should let your hand soak for awhile and I'll re-wrap it for you when you're done."

"Ummm. . .," Sophia ventured. "I. . .uh. . .need to. . .."

"Oh, of course! Abby, show Miss Sophia where the outhouse is."

It was when Abby helped her to stand that Sophia realized she wasn't wearing her own clothes. A soft, white cotton nightgown covered her down to her ankles. Mrs. Sampson seemed to read her face. "I took the liberty of washing your clothes. If you have any other clothing in your satchel, I'd be happy to wash those, too."

"Thank you." Sophia was embarrassed to have made this nice woman go out of her way so much to care for her. Back home, she was the one who had always had to help take care of Hisham. She wasn't used to being cared for. Especially by a stranger!

Abby led Sophia outside into the warm morning. The light hurt her eyes at first and she had to blink while they adjusted to the bright sun. She saw a round, wooden tub on the ground, with water still in it. Her clothes were hanging from a line that ran from the house to a wooden pole.

When they got to the outhouse, Sophia didn't know what to think. It was exactly like a real outhouse. Inside, the wooden bench was clean but the stench was unbearable. She did her business as fast as she possibly could and was relieved to find a small tin pail filled with water and a pile of leaves beside it that she could clean herself with. She had been afraid she would have to make do with a corn cob! She washed after relieving herself and tried to pat dry with a leaf from the pile. Then she rinsed her hands and escaped the dark, smelly confines of the toilet.

Abigail was waiting for Sophia when she emerged, and she walked her back to the house. She still hadn't said more than good morning. The sun was pretty high—it must have been close to noon—and there wasn't much of a breeze. When Sophia looked up and saw the house for the first time from the outside, she stopped in her tracks. It was a soddy. It was actually made of earth!

Like every schoolchild in the Great Plains, Sophia had studied the way the pioneers who settled the prairies had had to use the earth itself to build homes for themselves because trees grew only on riverbanks. She'd seen models of them and pictures of them, but she never thought she'd see one in actual use. As they stepped into the doorway, Sophia reached up and touched the outer wall to make sure it wasn't some sort of imitation sod, like football turf. Nope. The house was made of huge chunks of earth cut straight from the ground. They were about eight inches thick and still had the tangled roots of grass weaving through them.

Sophia was glad to be able to sink into the rocking chair inside. She didn't see any tourists or cameras or any other traces of modernity that would assure her that this was a living history camp. Sophia's mind raced and whirled. She had a

50

million questions for her hosts, but couldn't form any of them into words. Her hands were suddenly cold. She just sat and felt the unwelcome rush of panic as her chest tightened, her heart raced, and her breath became short. And unlike that night in Huda's house, this time she really had something substantial to be afraid of!

Mrs. Sampson placed the ceramic water basin in front of her on the floor and began to wash her hand. She had warmed the water a little and it felt soothing on Sophia's scraped palm. Then she bustled about getting lunch ready while Sophia sat in the chair, blinking her eyes and praying for the panic to recede so she could think clearly and decide how to approach Mrs. Sampson with all her questions.

Mrs. Sampson apologized for the meager meal. "Forgive me for not offering you a better spread, but Mr. Sampson didn't bring home any game yesterday. So we'll be eating bacon and some leftover prairie hen stew. That's what you really need, anyway, dear. Some good, thick stew. It's my special recipe. I got it from a woman whose wagon broke down on the way West and whose family stayed with us for a short while. I hope you like it. Where did you and your folks start out from, New York?"

As Sophia was trying to figure out how to decline the bacon without seeming rude, she had to quickly think of the answer to Mrs. Sampson's question. Her mind was so groggy and confused that it was harder than it should have been.

"Yes," she said, and didn't know why. She had been to New York once, when she and her mom had gone with her dad to a media conference. "We've. . .been staying in Kansas City for awhile, though."

"Oh, so they're callin' it Kansas CITY now?" Mrs. Sampson laughed. "Boston is a city. New York is a city. Kansas Town's just a glorified campsite." Seeing the look on Sophia's face she added more gently, "Well, I suppose it'll be a city someday. Where were you planning on homesteading?"

Sophia looked closely at Mrs. Sampson, trying to discern whether she was acting or if her questions were sincere. She didn't look like she was playing some sort of role. She looked earnest and interested. Sophia decided to buy some time. "We're not sure. . ..we're' just looking for a good place." She was beginning to believe she really was in 1857. Either that or these people were completely out of their minds. Or she was.

Mrs. Sampson spoke again, "I guessed you were from New York because your clothes are store-bought and I've never seen those fashions before. I was raised in Boston." Mrs. Sampson got a dreamy look on her face. "Sometimes I still miss it." Then, she waved away the thought lest it depress her. She turned back to her cooking.

Sophia wanted desperately to ask what year it

was, but she didn't want Mrs. Sampson to think she was crazy. The pit of her stomach was cold with fear. Maybe, somehow, she really was in 1857? She thought of asking Abby, but she hadn't said a word to Sophia and was quietly helping her mother get lunch together.

By now the stew was heated up and the bacon was set on the table. It hadn't been cooked, so Sophia assumed that it was also leftover, and that they ate it just like that. Eeeewww. She had seen her grandparents eat pepperoni on pizza but she still couldn't get used to the idea that people actually ate pigs. Mrs. Sampson called Joshua in from where he had been playing in front of the house, and Abby set tin plates and cups around the table.

"You can use Mr. Sampson's plate," Mrs. Sampson said.

Sophia took a long sniff of her stew. Nothing had ever smelled so good. She didn't want to be impolite, but she was so starving that she could hardly wait to begin eating. When Abby finally came to the table after washing her hands in the water left from the morning's clothes washing, Mrs. Sampson asked Joshua to say the grace. The family took hands, including Sophia's. Joshua prayed quickly, "Dear Father, we thank you for this food. Please bless it to our bodies and our bodies to thy service. Amen."

"Amen," agreed Mrs. Sampson. "Amen," Sophia

added.

The stew was every bit as good as it smelled, and the cornbread Mrs. Sampson gave Sophia to sop it up with was tasty and filling. When the bacon was passed to her, Sophia simply demurred, saying, "No thank you. I don't eat pork."

A look of understanding passed over Mrs. Sampson's face. "Umm, if I may be so impolite as to pose the question, Miss Sophia. . .are you Jewish?"

Sophia was startled. "No." She responded before she could think. "I'm a Muslim." Then she wished she had said she was Jewish. They probably didn't even know what a Muslim was.

Their reaction confirmed that theory. They just looked at her blankly. Mrs. Sampson was graceful in her recovery, though. "Oh, well, we do have all types of people here on the prairie. We ourselves are Christians – Methodists. I have not met any Muslims as of yet, but we have neighbors who are from Belgium, and Germany and even Mexico! And there are Indian tribes, also." When she saw the startled look on Sophia's face, she added, "We have very good relations with them. There isn't as much violence as there used to be." Her speech patterns were polite and very formal, and yet she made Sophia feel comfortable and at ease. Mrs. Sampson went on, "I wondered if you were Jewish when I saw your scarf last night, because my sister Ulianne lives in Chicago, and she writes to me of all the different groups of people there. She said the Jewish women dress like the Virgin Mary, and that they are always kind and modest, and make wonderful food."

"We have some Jewish neighbors back home, and they are very nice. Their mom sends us cakes and sweets she makes." Then, not wanting to have to offer any more details about her home, Sophia changed the subject. "Speaking of good food, this stew is delicious."

"Oh, please, have some more," Mrs. Sampson insisted, even though there wasn't much left in the heavy iron pot. She scooped the last bit into Sophia's plate. Normally Sophia wouldn't have dreamed of taking the last bit of food, but her hunger won out over her manners, and she ate the stew gratefully. When she finished she tried to help Abby clear the table.

"Oh, no you don't," scolded Mrs. Sampson. "You have to let yourself heal. I'll do the dishes and then we'll wrap your hand up again." Abby took the dishes out to the tub that had earlier been used for the clothing and Mrs. Sampson used a rag dipped in the soapy water to wipe the dishes clean. Sophia cringed. That was the same water they had used to wash her clothes! It was probably teeming with germs by now.

Sophia wanted to make ablution for prayer before her hand was wrapped up again, but considering the multi-purpose tub she thought clean water might be difficult to come by. She decided to make *tayamum*—emergency dry ablution. She plucked up her courage. "Mrs. Sampson, do you mind if I pray here next to the bed?

If Mrs. Sampson was curious about Sophia's faith, her manners must have kept her from asking any questions. "Of course, dear. I'll go see if your clothes are dry.

Sophia didn't know if she really needed to do that or if she was just inventing an excuse to go outside and give her guest some privacy. Either way, she was thankful.

Sophia found her backpack leaning next to the bed. Her compass still worked, thank God, because she was completely turned around. She found the *Qibla* and lay her rug on the bare earth floor facing the northeast, while Mrs. Sampson helped Abby with the last of the dishes. After her ritual prayer, Sophia begged Allah to get her back to her parents. Everyone fantasizes about going back in time, but thinking it might really be happening to you was another matter completely. She felt, above anything else, guilt. Guilt that she had been so careless as to fall down the bank and that now she couldn't reach her parents. Her mother would be frantic and sick with worry. Sophia knew that all things happen by the will of Allah, but she couldn't shrug off the heavy weight of her conscience.

She was also worried that she was hallucinating. She wasn't sure which would be worse – for all this to be real or for her to be losing her mind. She determined to go ahead and ask Mrs. Sampson the date as soon as she was finished praying.

Sophia was exhausted by the time she said "*Amin*," and Mrs. Sampson came back in with her clean clothes. Just as she was opening her mouth to ask the date, Joshua began jumping up and down outside. "Pa, Pa!!" he yelled. And sure enough, his pa's and Mr. Bodine's horses were just coming into view across the prairie.

Mrs. Sampson handed Sophia her clothes, and she was able to dress and don her scarf before the men rode up to the house. They were dusty and their faces were drawn. Jacques rode in on Emily, who was now empty of furs, and Mr. Sampson on a majestic black horse, much sleeker than the old mare.

As they slid out of their saddles, the men looked at Sophia. Mrs. Sampson gave her husband a "go easy" look, and he began tentatively. "I'm sorry, Miss Sophia," he apologized, "we weren't able to locate your folks. We rode to Independence and Westport, and even to Chouteau's Landing. No one on any of the wagon trains has reported a missing young lady."

As Mr. Sampson spoke, Sophia felt the last puzzle piece fall into place.

She really was in 1857.

She was astounded but, thankfully, the panic did not return. She just suddenly knew that if Allah had willed this strange detour in the force of time, then there must be an amazingly good reason, and He must be taking care of everything else. She wondered if this happened to other people, too, but they just never talked about it.

With the certain knowledge of her situation, Sophia's heart settled down. She just suddenly, miraculously, knew that her parents would be OK. Her feelings of guilt lifted and she felt lighter, even with the gravity of being stuck in the past.

"You can't imagine the chaos in town," Mr. Sampson continued. "There are steam boats arriving with hundreds of people, everyone trying to purchase supplies, book passage on stage coaches, establish land claims—it's insanity. Thank God we came out when we did, Eleanor. Anyway, we left placards around announcing that we had found you, and took out an ad in the Lawrence *Herald of Freedom*. Your folks will probably pass by Lawrence on their way West and, if so, hopefully they'll see the advertisement." Sophia knew they wouldn't. "But to tell you the truth, what I'm afraid of is that they believe you were washed away for good."

Me, too, thought Sophia. She felt a rush of warmth for this good-hearted family. She was grateful to Mr. Sampson for trying so hard—taking an entire day off of whatever work it was that he usually did to try and find her family. "Thank you, Mr. Sampson. I appreciate your kindness," she managed to tell him.

"Well, dear, you'll just stay with us until your family comes back for you, assuming they see the advertisement in Lawrence," Mrs. Sampson said, as if that closed the matter. And as far as Sophia was concerned, it did. Where else could she go?

"Thank you, Mrs. Sampson," she said. "I'll do my best to help out in whatever way I can."

Jacques lightened the mood. "Mrs. Sampson, we had a very poor meal in Westport. You happen to have anythin' we could refresh ourselves with?"

"Oh, of course, forgive me!" bustled Mrs. Sampson. "I have some bacon and cornbread. Joseph, did you bring the molasses?"

"Yes I did! And I got you a little surprise, too." Mr. Sampson went to his horse and got two items from his saddlebag. One was a ceramic jug of molasses and the other was a small crystal bowl. Mrs. Sampson opened its lid and found it was full of white sugar. "I thought since we had company and all. . ."

Mrs. Sampson smiled at her husband. "Oh, Joseph, you shouldn't have!" But it was obvious she was glad he had. She put the cornbread, bacon, and a small pitcher of the molasses on the table, and the men ate it all up in five minutes flat.

Later that night, Sophia and Abby and Joshua went to bed behind a quilt hung across the room, dividing the big bed she had slept on the night before from the "kids' room." Their mattress was a trundle bed that pulled out from under their parents' bed.

Mrs. Sampson had moved a few blankets from the trunk, and that gave Sophia a private space in which to keep her backpack and her one change of clothes. As she lay on the crowded but comfy feather mattress, Sophia felt something tickling at the edge of her mind. Something that had bothered her about the day's events that she couldn't quite remember. She recited from the Qur'an the verses Muslims say before bed, and turned over to sleep, dismissing whatever it was. Then suddenly it popped clearly into her head. Both Mr. Sampson and Jacques had worn pistols in holsters on each hip. And they had not taken them off—even when they had come in to eat.

7

THAT FIRST WEEK ALTERNATELY flew and dragged by, as Sophia's wounds healed and she got used to her new surroundings. Her hand healed a lot more quickly than she would have expected, and Sophia wondered what was in the ointment that Mrs. Sampson gave her to apply to it when she changed her bandages. The goose egg on her head remained as a bruise but she didn't suffer any more dizziness or nausea from it. Her shoes tightened from having been wet and she couldn't squeeze into them anymore, so she gave up and went barefoot like Abby, Josh, and Mrs. Sampson.

Not taking a shower every day was one of the hardest things to get used to. That, and the bugs. It was as if bugs were part of the family. Sadie had fleas. Mosquitoes were active in the evenings— actually moving in swarms down closer to the river—and chiggers dwelt in the prairie grasses.

After the first two days, Sophia gave up on rubbing hydrocortisone cream into her bites. No one else seemed to even notice the bugs. Sophia prayed she wouldn't get malaria (which, it turned out, was the mysterious "ague") or West Nile or Lyme disease—did they even have West Nile in 1857?

The sounds of the prairie were another thing Sophia had to acquaint herself with. The wind was a constant companion and took many moods, sometimes refreshing, sometimes annoying, sometimes downright scary. The mating calls of prairie chickens startled Sophia as well. She imagined an entire gaggle of ghosts when she heard their unearthly "wwoooooo, wooo." Mrs. Sampson said they called it "booming" and assured her that they were harmless and that mating season was almost over.

As Sophia got familiar with her surroundings, she discovered that in addition to the outhouse, there was also a stable built of logs on the other side of the house, a small shed made of sod, and a deep well about 100 yards out the front door. She was glad about the well; it meant fresh, clean water without having to trek all the way to the river, and she didn't have to worry about using extra water to make her ablutions before prayer. But she asked Abby why the stable was made of logs while the house was made of sod. It seemed backwards. Abby said that horse thieves were everywhere in the territory. Her dad had dragged the logs from the river bank to make the stable because if they lost their animals they wouldn't be able to live. There would be no way to till the soil, no transportation, and no milk!

"Besides," she explained, "sod holds in the heat in the winter and holds out the heat in the summer. Log cabins are drafty and cold," she said. This was the longest conversation they had had. Abby just didn't talk much. She wasn't unfriendly, but she certainly didn't seem like she wanted to bond with Sophia, either.

Sophia also asked Mrs. Sampson about the men's pistols and the shotgun that hung next to the door of the little soddy. Mrs. Sampson answered that on the frontier everyone had guns. She said that that had bothered her when they had first arrived, too. It seemed so uncivilized. But the fact was that prairie life was dangerous. A man could meet a wolf, a hostile Indian, a horse thief, or even a cougar at any moment. She said that nowadays land squatters were also becoming a danger. Unscrupulous men would come in from the East, plant a stake in part of someone else's land, and then defend it to the death as if it were theirs. In this way many innocent homesteaders and guilty squatters had been killed recently, so everyone was extra vigilant. She told Sophia that the men usually carried rifles in scabbards on their horses in addition to their pistols. She even shocked Sophia by adding that when she went out to the fields alone, as she sometimes had to do, she took a gun with her as well. Sophia couldn't imagine it. Mrs. Sampson seemed so delicate and proper.

Mrs. Sampson mended Sophia's torn scarf and gave her one of her sunbonnets, which Sophia discovered made a perfect head covering. The quilt was an amazingly good room divider, too, and Sophia wasn't uncomfortable sleeping in technically the same room with the adults, although sleeping with Joshua on the other side of Abby took some getting used to. She was too tired and sore at the end of every day to care much about such things, though—or to be anxious, usually. She just melted into the mattress and slept.

Morning came early on the prairie. She and Abby had to rise before the dawn prayer to milk the Sampsons' three cows: Rosey, Tinker, and Jo-Jo. Abby taught Sophia to do this and it was the only time Sophia had seen her laugh. She got a huge kick out of Sophia's city-girl squeamishness when she'd first reached out to milk the teat. Little did she know that Sophia was really wondering if you could get mad cow disease or some equally insidious illness from the cow's undersides.

The Sampsons were very kind about her prayers and porkless diet. They never mentioned it after that first day, and never offered her bacon or salt-pork, although these things were a staple of their own diets. They had family worship every evening, and at first Sophia was worried about that. But as it turned out, the Bible stories they read, about Prophet Noah or Prophet Moses, even Prophet Jesus, all contained admonishments to worship God and not let other things come ahead of that. Sophia was rather shocked that there were so many precise similarities between Christianity and Islam.

After a while, she became comfortable enough to add things that she knew about the Prophets, and this let the Sampsons also begin to understand the similarities between their faiths. At first, they had been afraid that Sophia worshipped cows or trees or something, so finding out that she worshipped God was a relief for them. Once Mr. Sampson asked her to read aloud from "her Bible" (they had seen her reading her little Qur'an several times). She recited part of the chapter called "Yusuf," the story of Prophet Joseph, and they were impressed that she knew Arabic and could recite her scripture in its original language. None of them had ever met a Christian who could recite the Old Testament in Hebrew or the New Testament in Greek.

Sophia joined Abby in all her chores, and tried to ignore the blisters and aching muscles that were the result. The girls lugged water from the well and washed clothes in the tub with a scrub board and homemade lye soap, which Sophia found so strong she felt reassured that it would kill any germs lingering from either their clothes or the bacon fat. They swept the earthen floor twice a day, milked the cows, churned butter, and tended the garden, which Mr. Sampson had plowed up with the help of his black horse, who Sophia learned was named Othello. The Sampsons also had a brown and white mare named Ophelia. Sophia was impressed that they knew Shakespeare. She began to see that Mrs. Sampson especially was very educated.

Sophia was in awe of Eleanor Sampson's skills, as well. That spring she mended clothes, sewed a set of curtains, made a barrel of homemade vinegar, dried and mixed herbs for medicines, and dipped candles. All that in addition to her regular chores of making bread and butter, cooking, keeping the house and tending the garden.

Mr. Sampson took his two oxen out every day—always wearing his pistols—and usually came back so exhausted that Joshua or Mrs. Sampson had to take his boots off for him. He had used the oxen to plow his own fields—more land each year was devoted to fields—but now he was taking them every day to their Belgian neighbor, Mr. Kerkhoff, to help him clear stumps and boulders from his land so he could plant wheat in the fall. In exchange, Mr. Kerkhoff's son sent small game he had hunted to the Sampsons just about every other day for three weeks. Sophia and the Sampsons ate prairie hens, venison, squirrel, quail, and rabbits. It was like attending a free meat buffet every day.

There weren't many vegetables, though, except for onions, tomatoes that Mrs. Sampson had put up the year before, dried turnips, and a few early radishes. For vegetables, they would have to wait until the garden started to yield its crop. But there was always fresh-baked cornbread or biscuits to eat. Sophia learned quickly how to moisten the corn meal to the right consistency or warm the yeast to just the right temperature, and she became the official family bread maker. Back home, she had only seen bread made once, and that was the flat Arabic pita bread kind. She wondered if her new skills would be transferred back home with her. . .if she was ever transferred back.

The thought of home was with her day and night. Sometimes, if she could get time alone hanging laundry or milking the cows, she would allow the tears to come. She missed her family, especially her mom, and she missed being around other Muslims. She tried to figure out what mechanism had taken her a century and a half away from her home. She wondered if maybe she had been caught in some one-way wormhole, and if Allah had simply willed that she be stuck here in 1857 for the rest of her life. She had to believe, though, that Allah had arranged this time anomaly for a specific purpose, and she was always looking for some reason, some task that appeared to have her name on it.

But so far no great calling had presented itself, and Sophia was left saying *alhamdulillah* for everything, even though she didn't really feel very grateful for her predicament. She hoped, most of all, that time was not moving for her family. That her family had not really, as Mr. Sampson suggested, come to believe that she had been washed away. She couldn't bear the thought that her parents were grieving, thinking her dead. She prayed that Allah wouldn't allow that.

The hunting arrangement Mr. Sampson had with Mr. Kerkhoff left him some free time to go buy lumber in town once the Kerkhoff's clearing was finished. The Sampsons were preparing to build a real frame house on their land. It would have two separate bedrooms upstairs and a kitchen and a living room downstairs. And glass windows—at least one in each room. Abby was more excited about the windows than anything else, and Sophia could see why. Living with just the wax paper-covered hole in the soddy made for dark, depressing conditions.

When the lumber was brought in, Mr. Sampson began constructing the inner walls of the downstairs. Sophia was shocked at how fast it went. Sometime soon they would have a house-raising, where several men from the surrounding community would come and help Mr. Sampson put up the outer walls of the house all in one day. Sophia was amazed that this could be done and couldn't wait to see it.

One afternoon, about two weeks after Sophia had dragged herself up out of the Kansas river and into a new world, she had taken the kitchen table outside and was kneading dough on it when Joshua came out from the house with something in his hand. Sophia liked Joshua. He was cheerful and talkative—not dour and quiet like Abby—and seemed to want more than anything to grow up and be a man. He was always whittling weapons or farm tools out of wood with his pocketknife, of which he was extremely proud, and often talked about what he was doing as he did it. Sophia found his chatter comforting. Sometimes he asked her to hold a stick or peel some bark off of a branch and she was glad to help him. He reminded her of Hisham and gave her something to concentrate on besides worrying about her situation. It occurred to her that she was nicer to Joshua than she had ever been to her own brother. She vowed that if she should ever get home she'd treat her brother better.

When she looked up and saw what was in Joshua's hand, her heart skipped a beat. It was her cell phone.

The Sampson's had always been very careful about her privacy, and Sophia had never worried about her things. She had thought several times of telling them the truth of where she came from, and knew that eventually she probably would. They had been respectful of her need to be left alone, but there were so many times when it would just be natural to tell a story about her dad's computer or Amani's driving antics. Sophia felt weird having to edit the things she mentioned about her family all the time, and she wished she could just come completely clean. She certainly wasn't prepared to do it today, though.

"Sophia?" Josh asked, "What's this?" Then, seeing the startled look on her face, he went on hastily, "I wasn't snoopin', honest. I was just lookin' at that bzzzzzzz thing that closes your bag—I wanted to make one for my marble bag—and this fell out of the pocket."

Sophia thought quickly. She used her literature teacher's favorite tactic. She turned the question back on him. "What do *you* think it is, Josh?"

"I think it's one of those telegraph senders! Can I try it?"

"It's not mine, Josh. It's my dad's." Well, it was true. Her dad paid the cell phone bill, so technically it was his. "Can you put it back, please? I don't want it to get broken. In case I do find my family someday, I don't want him to think I wasn't careful with it."

Josh did as he was asked and then came and sat in the doorway and worked on the bow he was making.

Sophia went on kneading the bread, but she was disconcerted. She could not figure out how to explain her real history to the Sampsons.

The preparations for the house raising began a week ahead of time. Mr. Sampson spent a good bit of time measuring the foundation of the house and its porch. Mrs. Sampson made sure that she and the girls' "Sunday best" clothes were clean and that everyone had taken baths the day before. They got up early that morning (even earlier than usual) and had all their regular chores done by shortly after sunup. They ate biscuits and molasses for breakfast and got dressed up. To Sophia, this was like dressing up to go work at a carwash or something, but Mrs. Sampson said they had to retain some sort of dignity in front of the neighbors. After all, they were not common ruffians. They were well-bred Easterners, and had to maintain decorum. Besides, she said, this was the first time most of the neighbors would meet Sophia, and Mrs. Sampson wanted her to look nice. Sophia was thoroughly embarrassed when Mrs. Sampson insisted that she wear her own Sunday dress while Mrs. Sampson herself got an even fancier dress out of a trunk in the stable. Sophia was terrified she'd tear or stain the beautiful, flowing dress, which was made of heavy cotton and had several layers of petticoats under the skirt. But it fit her nicely, and Sophia's sunbonnet atop her braided bun completed the look.

The neighbors started to arrive shortly thereafter—entire families bearing food and tools. There were the Kerkhoffs, the family that had exchanged plowing for meat, the Edigars from near the river, and the Duncans, who had six children, one of whom was an orphaned Indian boy about Abby's age. Sophia saw him only briefly, as he took a blanket to the edge of the yard and sat alone. She wondered why he didn't go help the men. He was certainly old enough.

The Elys came with Matthew. They were newly married, and Mrs. Ely was exactly Sophia's age. She was so grown-up and mature that Sophia felt babyish next to her. She carried herself just like a real wife, as if being married at 16 were the most natural thing in the world. The food began to pile up and they had to set up the door for the new house across two wagon trunks outside for an extra table. There was fried chicken, stews flavored with dried berries, boiled eggs, biscuits, bowls of fresh butter, and cold roasted venison. There were canned tomatoes cooked with bread and spices, and one family even brought peppermint sticks for all the children.

Sophia was introduced all around, and was kept busy tending the little ones with Abby and helping Mrs. Sampson ready all the food for lunchtime, when the men would take a break from working on the house and everyone would eat together. Sophia had wondered how they would feed all those people, as the only dishes the Sampsons' had were the tin ones they ate on every day. Each person had his own plate and cup, except Sophia.

She ate on a wooden bucket lid and drank from a blue-green glass jar.

She didn't have to wonder about this for long, because as noon approached all the women went to their wagons and retrieved their own plates and utensils. They all spread out blankets on the ground around the front yard of the soddy and then Sophia and Abby were sent to call the menfolk. When they arrived at the house site, which was to the right as you came out the door of the soddy, close to the well, Sophia caught a glimpse of Matthew hammering a nail into a board at about arm level. She was shocked at the emotion that ran through her. The sight of that respectful, quiet, dignified young man, with his shirtsleeves rolled up and a look of concentration on his face, made her blush. She remembered the kind, concerned way he had cared for her that first night, and the way he looked down at his boots when they were introduced, out of deference to a lady. Sophia looked away and let Abby call the men. As soon as Abby had gotten the message across, Sophia turned and started to walk back to the soddy.

"Sophia!" panted Abby, as she caught up with Sophia's long, purposeful strides. "Why are you in such a hurry?" Of course Abby would choose now to begin being friendly. Sophia felt awkward and uncomfortable.

"I just wanted to get back and help your mom. We left her with all the guests."

"Oh, you're right." Now it was Abby's turn to look uncomfortable. She began speaking hesitantly. "My pa is going to town again this week, to get fixtures for the house. He said if we help him put them in, he'll get us a present from the general store. Is there anything you'd like to have?"

"Oh," gasped Sophia. "I don't want to put your pa to any trouble."

"It's no trouble." She looked down. "He knows you're going through a hard time and he wants to make you feel. . ." Abby paused. "L-like one of the family." Her last words rushed out as if she were afraid of them.

"Well. . ." Sophia thought of the things she had wished for over the past few weeks. Most of them were things they didn't have in 1857! Some M&M's, her computer, a washing machine and dryer. She *would* like a pair of shoes, but those seemed awfully expensive. Sophia hadn't even seen anyone in the Sampson family besides Mr. Sampson wearing shoes. She decided on something that was probably not too costly but that she'd wished for several times.

"I'd like some paper." Sophia had pencils and pens in her backpack, but she had taken her spiral notebooks out the night she'd stored her school books in her closet back home. She'd been longing to write about her experiences and her worries.

Abby looked at her as if truly seeing her for the first time. "Do you like to sketch?"

"No," answered Sophia truthfully. "I'm no good at it. But I like to write."

Abby didn't answer. The girls were almost at the soddy, but Sophia didn't want this first real conversation with Abby to end so soon. She had wondered what it was about her that Abby didn't like. She'd thought maybe Abby was jealous, or maybe she just wasn't a people person.

"What are you going to ask for?" she ventured.

Abby stopped walking and considered for a minute. "I think I'll ask for paper, too."

"Do you like to draw?"

"Yes. But I'm not very good at it, either," blushed Abby.

The girls had reached the soddy's yard, where the women were bustling about putting food onto plates for the small children. As the men caught up, they picked up their own plates and filled them with food from the tables. Then they went to the blankets spread out on the ground. At last the women took their food and everyone ate together in front of the small soddy.

Sophia was startled to hear someone addressing her from behind. "I'm so sorry to hear of your misfortune, Miss Sophia." It was Mrs. Jordan, a very refined looking lady who had arrived late at the house-raising with her husband and small son. She had a soft, velvety southern accent. "I do hope that Providence will reunite you with your family very soon. Your hostess tells me you are from New

York?"

"Thank you, Ma'am. Yes," she answered.

"We visited New York once. The river harbors were so busy I don't know how the ships get in and out without sinking each other."

"Sometimes the ships do run into each other," Sophia offered. It was probably true.

Mrs. Jordan's little boy came asking for more chicken. He was about three years old, and was dressed in little short pants that came just below his knees. He was the only boy there dressed like that, and from the looks of his mother's rather fancy store-bought dress—complete with bustle— his clothes must have been high fashion back East. Mrs. Jordan scolded him lovingly for interrupting adults when they were talking. She deboned a bit of a chicken leg for him, and then turned back to Sophia.

"You simply *must* pay us a visit, Miss Sophia. We just finished our house last fall, and it hasn't seen enough visitors. I enjoy company. It is one of the things I miss most about home."

"Where is your original home, Mrs. Jordan?" Sophia asked. She was charmed by this woman's kind bearing and manners.

"Atlanta, dear. My husband decided we should move here because there was so much opportunity. We want to be part of the founding generation of the new territory. And we also believe it is our duty to help ensure that when these territories become states, the rights of the states are respected by those vultures in Washington."

Sophia didn't understand all the vulture talk, but she felt sure she could understand the spirit that motivated the Jordans to explore and settle new territories, and she was glad that someone was thinking ahead enough to plan for protecting the rights of Kansans. Mrs. Jordan had vision; she was hoping that Kansas would prove to be a bustling, new, up-and-coming state, and if it did, she wanted her family to be looked up to by later arrivals and later generations, as those who had settled and founded the new state. Sophia wondered if many other pioneers had had such grandiose dreams. The Sampsons didn't seem to be concerned with stuff like that.

Even though Mrs. Jordan seemed a bit pretentious, Sophia liked her. She hoped she would be able to visit her home. Mrs. Jordan's son, who Sophia learned was named Samuel, returned with his empty plate.

"Ma, may I have a cake?"

"What do you say, dear?"

"Please."

"Good boy. Of course you may. Please excuse me, Miss Sophia." She got up to get him a piece of cake and stayed to visit with some of the other ladies around the table.

Sophia was wondering what these people would think if they knew that Kansas did turn out to be a real state, and that it was only in the middle of the United States! She was thinking about Alaska and Hawaii, and imagining the astonishment on the faces of the settlers if she told them that the US grew beyond its geographical borders like that. Sophia was grinning to herself with the thought of drawing them a map when her attention was distracted by fighting children.

A small group of young kids had gathered around the Indian boy. They were teasing him and some were even poking and kicking at him. He was just sitting on the ground eating, without showing any sign that he even noticed their torments. Sophia got up to investigate.

"Look, he's a wolf boy!"

"His Indian name should be 'Eats Like a Pig!'"

Sophia stepped between the children and the solemn young man, whose back was completely straight and whose face was entirely serene. She was hesitant to say anything to other people's children, especially when the people were complete strangers, but her indignation won out.

"Please, children," she begged in a hushed tone. "This is not polite. This boy is our guest." She was relieved when Mrs. Sampson came to reinforce her. Sophia had never seen her speak an irritated word to anyone, but she was firm with the Indian boy's tormentors.

"Boys and girls, your behavior is reflecting poorly on yourselves. I would appreciate it if you would not be rude to young Mr. Duncan."

The motley crew of youngsters grudgingly straggled away from the young Indian boy, but not before they gave him—and Sophia—looks of complete contempt.

Sophia was furious. When she and Amani had been in the fourth grade, there had been a boy who had attended their school for one year. His name was Bilal Sinai, but some of the kids had called him 'The Terrorist.' He didn't speak much English and had dark, brooding features. Sophia and Amani had protected him against one particular bully. Everyone felt sorry for Bilal, but only Sophia and Amani stood up for him.

That kind of thing infuriated her. How dare people think they had a right to make fun of others? She began to apologize to the boy and was shocked when she saw his face close-up. It was blotchy colored and severely scarred. It looked almost as if his face had been burned with cigarettes or something. She also realized that though he was facing the vast prairie, he wasn't staring off into the distance. He was blind. That must be why he wasn't helping the men. *SubhanAllah.* Sophia told him she was sorry that the children had bothered him. When he didn't respond, she wondered if he were deaf as well as blind. She finished her apology lamely and went back to her plate.

Sophia could not understand how the children could get away with picking on a handicapped person like that in broad daylight, when all the adults were close by.

Then she found out.

After the children had gone off and started a game of tag (which apparently they didn't consider half as fun as torturing innocent victims), Mrs. Edigar announced her opinion rather loudly. "I don't blame the children for making fun of that little redskin. Did you see the way he was eating, with his *hands*? They are so dirty."

"I don't mind the dirt so much as the stealing!" added a heavy-set woman that Sophia had not been introduced to. "It happened to me awhile back. One minute I was stirring stew, all alone except the kids, and when I turned around, there was this huge, ugly, stinking Indian already squatted on the floor behind me. I had to feed him the stew, AND he took the tobacco can and an armload of pelts that my Manfred had tanned. But of course there's nothing a settler can do, because if you fight back they'll come in the night and scalp you."

"They are always drunk and raisin' Cain in the city. I don't think they can be Christianized. They are just too heathen," said Mrs. Edigar, as she began picking up the plates from her family's blanket and taking them to soak in the big wash tub that had been set up for everyone to wash their dishes in.

Sophia was beside herself. She wanted to punch those women. She wanted to remind them that the

Indians had had their homes stolen from them, had been pushed farther and farther West, had been lied to and cheated by the white man, had been virtually wiped out by wars and disease and deception! She wanted to inform them that most Native American cultures had been very complex and civilized, and that even if they hadn't been, it certainly wasn't very "Christian" to treat the Indians the way the Americans had.

She appealed to Mrs. Sampson with a helpless look of fury, and Mrs. Sampson, in her quiet manner, spoke with her eyes. "We'll talk about it later, dear," her eyes said. Sophia looked at the dignified Indian boy, sitting near Mrs. Edigar's blanket on the ground all by himself. *Alhamdulillah* he was deaf – or maybe couldn't understand English. She vowed to help him in any way she could.

The rest of the day was long and difficult for Sophia. It was made bearable only by Mrs. Jordan's company, as they wiped the dishes together and stacked them so that each family could reclaim theirs. The leftover food—what little there was of it—was left out for the men to eat when they returned at sunset from the house-raising. When the dishes were cleared and the small children put down for naps inside on blankets covering the dirt floor, the ladies sat in a circle and brought out their sewing, embroidery or mending. Sophia busied herself making more bread for the supper. When that was done and there was no more excuse for avoiding the women, she went and sat with them. She took out her prayer beads, which she normally only used after prayer or when she was alone, and made *istighfar*, seeking forgiveness, while the other women chatted about children, crops and the new Methodist circuit pastor. Not all of them were Methodists, Mrs. Sampson explained later, but the Methodist preacher was the only one who came near enough and often enough for people to attend his services, so everyone went to them—Catholics, Baptists and Methodists alike.

As Sophia listened to their conversation she tried to make sense of the attitudes she had seen displayed that afternoon and to think of a way to help the Indian boy.

THAT EVENING, EVERYONE WAS far too
tired to talk about anything. But in the
morning Sophia asked Mrs. Sampson
about the Duncans' ward as the three
ladies shelled early peas from the garden. She
sensed that Mrs. Sampson felt the same way she
did about Mrs. Edigar's conversation, and she was
glad. Mrs. Sampson explained that some people on
the frontier were not educated or refined. She said
that these people judged the entire Redskin race
(Sophia couldn't believe she used that epithet!) by
the actions of a few.

"Of course, one can understand why people
would be cautious and prudent when it comes to
Redskins, but I can't abide it when folks assume
that the Indians can't be civilized. There are
several good, Christian Indians in this territory,
and I know many who are not Christian but who
are honorable, upright people. Their manners are

different from ours, but their hearts are not. They tend their crops, hunt their food, trade their beads and pelts, and cry when their children die, just like white people. And the ladies did not mention this yesterday, but they usually repay people when they take something. To them, it is not stealing, because. . .well, I'm not sure why. But they do not believe it to be a sin to take something, as long as they trade something else for it. That Indian who took Mrs. Schiller's husband's pelts and tobacco came back the next day, walked straight into her house, and left her some threaded beads, a basket of dried corn, and a pair of moccasins for each of her children.

"The real problem is that there are some evil settlers and some evil Indians. These few continue the violence and the rest of us have to live in fear because of them."

Sophia could relate to a situation like that. 9-11 had created a similar climate in her time, with some Americans fearing that any Muslim could be a terrorist and some Muslims fearing that any American could attack them in some sort of revenge hate crime. Of course the situation was the same, though, that only a few crazy people on either side were violent. Unfortunately, just as with the Native American wars, most of the victims on each side were innocent people just trying to live their lives.

To Sophia's shock, Abby joined the conversation.

"Ma went to the Kiowa village last winter when the smallpox was going around. She saved many of them."

"Abby, dear," said her mother gently, "We do not save people. God saves them. He decides when the angel of death shall visit each of us."

"Hmph," Abby grunted, and Sophia was shocked a second time.

"Adoeet's—that's the Duncan's boy's name— Adoeet's mother and scores of other Kiowa died in that go-round with the pox. That's why he is blind. He survived, but not unscathed."

Abby got up rather pointedly and went outside. "Why didn't he stay with his tribe?"

"Well, even though there wasn't a large epidemic of the smallpox last year in general, Adoeet's tribe was hit hard. They were almost devastated— there are only about 200 of them left. They lost so many people that they can hardly maintain themselves. And the people who were left were all in mourning. There was no way they could take care of him, especially with his handicap. So he stayed with us for awhile until the Duncans came forward and volunteered to care for him. They have a frame house with more bedrooms, and their eldest are boys."

Sophia thanked Allah again that she had wound up with the Sampsons and not some other family. She felt like hugging Mrs. Sampson—so she did, and Mrs. Sampson hugged her back.

Sophia almost cried, the gesture made her miss her mother so badly.

"We lost our own little Olivia to the smallpox this winter," Mrs. Sampson confided quietly, looking toward the door to make sure that Abby wasn't coming back in. "She was only two years younger than Abigail and was the apple of her eye. Abby's best friend Margaret also passed away last summer, when a team of horses ran away with the wagon while she was still in it. It overturned on her and she was crushed. Abigail has taken these things very hard, and is doubting Providence. She's angry because she sees it as unfair, and she's afraid to get close to people anymore, for fear they will be snatched away from her. That's one of the reasons I'm so glad that God saw fit to land you in our midst. I'm hoping that she'll open up to you."

Understanding dawned on Sophia and she saw Abby in a completely new light. It wasn't that she didn't like Sophia; it was just that her heart was scarred. To look at Mrs. Sampson, you would never guess that *her* life was so hard, that her heart was so full of tragedy and disappointment and sadness. She carried on with unshakeable faith in God, just as any good Muslim should do. Mrs. Sampson didn't let despair rule her.

When Abby came back in, Sophia took a long look at her. Now that she understood Abby's aloof demeanor, she vowed to try harder to befriend her.

"Well, ladies, let's get lunch going," said

Mrs. Sampson cheerfully, lifting the sad, foggy atmosphere in the little house and returning it to normal. They went about the lunch business quietly, though, each lost in her own thoughts.

When Mr. Sampson came in for dinner, they all sat down to a meal of roast turkey with the early peas. Mrs. Sampson had boiled them and then slathered them with butter. They were delicious, and Sophia didn't normally even like peas! But now she was so glad to have a vegetable—any vegetable—that she relished each one as it popped open in her mouth.

"I'll be making that run into Westport tomorrow," said Mr. Sampson. "Is there anything we need?"

"Will you be taking the wagon, Joseph?" asked Mrs. Sampson. "Yes, but we won't have much room. We'll have to carry all the windows and fixtures back with us."

"Well, we're almost out of salt. We need flour and such as well, but those can wait until next time."

"Pa, please bring me more peppermint candy like Edward's pa brought us at the house raisin'!" begged Joshua.

"Sophia and I would like some paper, Pa," put in Abby very quietly.

Sophia was embarrassed all over again. "You've done so much for me already," she said. "I hate to put you to any trouble."

"Nonsense," retorted Mr. Sampson jovially. "You're one of the family now, at least for the time being. And we're happy to have you as such. Paper it is."

"Thank you, Mr. Sampson."

"No trouble at all, dear," assured Mrs. Sampson again.

Mr. Sampson added, "You'll be drawin' or cipherin' or writing' up a storm come tomorrow evening!"

After dinner, while Sophia and Abby were doing the dishes, Mr. Sampson went out into the yard and set up a horseshoe "pitch." It was the first time Sophia had ever seen him do anything recreational. So far, he had always been in the fields or working on the house, from sunup to sundown as far as Sophia could tell. He was an expert at ringing the horseshoes around the stake, which was placed in the ground about 20 or 30 feet away from him. He let the children try, also, even though Mrs. Sampson was mortified. She insisted that playing horseshoes was NOT a ladylike pursuit. Abby was even willing to try, especially after her ma had expressed disapproval, and she and Sophia were equally bad, but Joshua shocked them all by ringing two in a row. Everyone laughed at the girls' pathetic attempts, and everyone cheered for Joshua. For the first time, Sophia felt like she was getting to know the Sampsons and really fitting in with the family. Up until now she had felt like a complete charity case.

The next day dragged by. Mr. Sampson was up and ready by the time the girls finished the milking, and Sophia thanked him quickly and shyly before he left. "I don't know what I'd have done if I hadn't wound up with your family," she stuttered.

Mr. Sampson's beard blew in the morning breeze. He comfortably downplayed her embarrassment and his family's deed, as he continued hitching the horses without even looking up. "Aww, it's nothin', Miss Sophia. Yer family'd do the same if the situation were reversed, I'm sure of it." Sophia smiled. She imagined Abby stranded in the 21st century, and thought how much better she'd fit in with a Muslim family than a non-Muslim one.

ᐧᐧᐧ

The girls got all their regular chores done early and then shelled some more peas. These were not for eating; they were for drying—to be eaten in the winter. By the time they were finished, a little while after lunch, their hands ached. Sophia washed hers in the dish tub and dried them on her apron as she walked outside for a break. She was in remarkably good shape these days, the weary ache of the sissy muscles that she had arrived with having given way to lean, efficient strength and stamina. Now, sitting for that long is what made her sore!

As she walked out of the soddy, she sensed a difference in the wind. It was blowing purposefully from the West and felt electric. She glanced up to where it was coming from and was greeted by an approaching wall of clouds, arriving from the southwest. It hadn't really rained much since Sophia had arrived, almost a month ago, now. A few showers here and there, but nothing serious. She watched the gathering clouds and breathed in the expectant air. "It looks like it's gonna storm," she yelled over her shoulder, and Mrs. Sampson came out to join her.

The chickens hopped excitedly, dashing into their small coop and running back out again, as if to check and see whether the rain had started yet. The insects interrupted their buzzing for short periods—feeling and listening for the coming storm. The clouds were deep, dark gray, almost blue, and Sophia was nervous. *At least they're not green*, she thought to herself. Greenish clouds were what people always talked about when they told stories of tornadoes.

Mrs. Sampson asked Abby to go bring the cows in from their tether line, where they had been grazing near the soddy since Mr. Sampson wasn't home. She had Sophia gather all the bowls, pots, and cups in the house and from the stable, and she placed them around the room in random-seeming spots. She herself brought in the laundry that had been hanging on the line.

"I sure hope Joseph makes it back before the rain starts," she fussed. "He's gone East, and he may not even know this is coming. That means he'll drive straight into it."

But the rain arrived before he did. At first it was just driving sprinkles. Not the kind that dance on your face or your windshield every second or two (Sophia was amazed to find that even the thought of windshields was foreign to her now), but the kind that arrive like little darts, piercing your clothes and stinging your skin. Then the lightening flashed and the thunder arrived just a second later, and a second or two after that, the rain opened up in earnest. With the animals safe in the stable and the laundry already inside, there was nothing to do but watch the storm.

Mrs. Sampson was nervous, too—not for herself but for Mr. Sampson. She stoked the fire in the stove, which they usually only fired up for cooking, since it was summer, and put the heavy iron on top of one of the flat, griddle-like burners. Sophia offered to do the ironing for her, but she insisted on doing it herself. She wanted to keep busy.

Soon the lightning and the thunder were occurring at almost the same exact instant. Sophia and Joshua stood at the door and watched the brilliant white streaks reaching all the way to the ground. Abby stayed at the kitchen table, busying herself with washing the peas. When Sophia asked her to come to the door, she said she was "afeared" of storms. Sophia was "afeared" as well, since the soddy didn't have a root cellar. The Sampsons stored their winter provisions in the small sod shed instead of underground. Then she remembered that Mr. Sampson had been digging a root cellar near the frame house. She'd wondered why they'd need it there, since when they moved they'd have the soddy to store things in, but she was glad it was there, nonetheless. The wind was getting fiercer by the minute.

The rain pelted the strong little soddy almost straight-on. As Sophia and Joshua watched, a prairie hen was swooped unceremoniously across the yard. It was trying to fly into the wind, but the wind had other ideas, and it wound up sailing head over heels back the way it had come. Sophia fretted some, but soon relaxed a bit. Once you've been swept across time, being carried off by a tornado isn't so daunting, she decided.

After about a half-hour, when the storm seemed to be blowing itself out and the rain was less driven but still pouring, water started leaking from the hay and sod roof. Amazingly, it began dripping in dirty little rivulets exactly into the containers Mrs. Sampson had placed. One of them was even right in the middle of the bed! Then all three of the children were kept busy emptying the small containers into a pitcher and tossing the brown water from the pitcher out the door. It was when they were doing this that they spotted Mr.

Sampson's wagon arriving from the east. And Matthew was with him.

The two soaking men drove the wagon up to the house and unhitched the horses. Matthew took them to the stable, while Mr. Sampson began unloading the things from the wagon that would be damaged by staying wet. He brought in the bag of salt he had purchased for Mrs. Sampson first. It had been strategically placed underneath the windows, so was only wet at one corner, and Mrs. Sampson was able to open it and take out the wet part. She didn't throw it away, but rather put it in one of the tin plates. She said she would use it to make pickles with, since the first cucumbers were almost ripe.

Soon Matthew joined Mr. Sampson, and they brought in a few more supplies, drying the wet ones with a blanket, before Mrs. Sampson could convince them to worry about themselves. Each of them was soaked to the bone and beginning to shiver. Sophia was glad Mrs. Sampson had done that ironing—the house was toasty warm, even though the air was now cooled from the rain. People on the prairie seemed to know how to plan things so as to the get best use out of everything!

The quilt was hung and Mrs. Sampson gave both the men clean trousers to wear. Mr. Sampson put on his nightshirt and gave Matthew a work shirt. When Matthew emerged from behind the blanket, his cheeks were red and his wet hair stood straight up. He looked thoroughly embarrassed, and Sophia thought he was the most handsome man she had ever seen. His very presence seemed calm and serious and responsible. He was a far cry from the boys in her class back at school, who usually presented no temptation for a young lady, because they only worried about what excuse to use for not turning in their homework *this time*, and they spent all their free time playing video games or throwing footballs around. She turned around straight away and began putting together the batter for some johnnycakes, while Mrs. Sampson served the men some hot tea she had put on while she had been ironing the clothes.

"Oh, Joseph, you two are going to catch your death!" To Sophia's dismay, she deposited the protesting men right next to the stove, so they could warm up. They insisted they were not in need of such care, but she would have none of it. She made them sit, and even brought out the white sugar for their tea. Sophia moved her batter to the table, so she was behind Matthew's back. She sat herself down in the chair and faced the other way. When it was time to put the batter into the heavy iron skillet to bake she did so, but she asked Mrs. Sampson to put it in the oven. Then she went to the edge of the bed to sit down. Suddenly the little house seemed far too small. She wished for some mending or something to do with her hands.

Soon Matthew stood up. "Well, Mrs. Sampson,

the rain's pretty much let up. Thank you for the tea. I need to be off."

"Oh, Matthew, you have to stay for some supper!" Mrs. Sampson insisted.

"I'd love to, Ma'am," Matthew replied. "But I've got to tend the cows. Old Jacques was goin' to bring 'em in for me, but his rheumatism acts up when it rains, and since we're back in time, I don't want him to have to do it." Then he looked straight at Sophia and dipped his head slightly. "Evenin', Miss Sophia."

Sophia's cheeks burned. "Evenin'," she stammered, as casually as she could. What was wrong with her? She had never felt or acted this nervous—like one of those silly seventh graders she and the other girls had had to mentor last year. Matthew stepped out into the early evening, tall and straight and completely at ease. Mr. Sampson went with him and saddled up one of the horses for him, so he wouldn't have to walk home. As the men moved away from the house, Sophia noticed a brilliant rainbow off above the stable.

After dinner that night, Mr. Sampson brought out a package of several items in an old burlap sack. He reached in and brought out two peppermint sticks for Joshua, and a wooden top with a string wrapped around it. Sophia would have thought that Joshua was a bit old for such a toy, but this top was cool. It took real skill to pull the string just right so that the top spun. Even Sophia herself couldn't do it on the first couple of tries. The second present Mr. Sampson brought out was a brass teapot for Mrs. Sampson. It had a rather pretentious etching of a peacock on one side, and a wooden handle. Mrs. Sampson was overjoyed, and said she wouldn't use it until they moved into the new house. Sophia thought she even saw a tear shining in her eye. Mr. Sampson gave Abby a shallow box of gray, rectangular paper, along with a large nub of lead to sketch with. The box said, "Big Chief" on it in red and black letters, just like the tablets Sophia remembered from her own childhood. Sophia assumed the paper was for the girls to share, but Mr. Sampson turned to her next.

She was shocked when he pulled from the package not a few sheets of paper, or even a notebook, but a bound, wooden journal, and handed it to her. As she looked at the beautiful book in her hands, she couldn't even speak. It had a tan wooden cover and a darker back cover, bound together with three loops of thick string. The front wood was stained and the word "Journal" was burned into the light-colored wood in fancy cursive writing. The paper was thickish and unlined. It was brown, like a paper sack from a grocery store, and had rough edges. The side edges of the journal were dusted with a gold color, and there was a small quill-type pen hanging from a cloth ribbon attached to the top left corner of the wood cover. It had to have cost a fortune. Even Sophia could tell that.

She looked up at Mr. Sampson with gratitude and amazement. "Oh, Mr. Sampson!" she exclaimed. "I. . .I don't know what to say. This is really too much. . .please let me trade with Abby!"

"Nope, can't let ya do that. That there diary's from Matthew," Mr. Sampson replied, obviously enjoying the reaction this elicited from Sophia. If Sophia had been shocked before, now she was flabbergasted. She turned the journal over and over in her hands, flipped through its pages and looked back at Mr. Sampson. Then she stammered, "Are you sure?"

"'Course! When I said you had asked for paper, he insisted on buying that. He said you looked like a writer to him. I think he must have taken a shine to you," he winked.

Sophia looked again at the journal in her lap. She didn't know what to think or say. She looked at Abby, who raised her eyebrows up and down at her. Joshua sang with a peppermint stick in his mouth, "Sophia's got a sweetheart! Sophia's got a sweetheart!"

Mrs. Sampson came to her rescue. "Joshua Sampson. That will be enough of that. If Mr. Collins is kind enough to buy a gift for Sophia, that doesn't mean he is her sweetheart." She turned her soft eyes upon Sophia. "That is a very nice gift, dear. And Matthew seems like a wonderful boy, although he hasn't been in the territory very long." She had reprimanded Joshua, but her own eyes shone with motherly mischief.

Sophia glanced down. "Yes, he does." She smiled before she could catch herself.

That night before Sophia turned in, she looked once more at the journal, feeling its pages and thumbing through them—inhaling the scent of new paper and the stain on the wood. As the pages fell into place, she noticed writing at the top of the first one. "To Miss Sophia," it read in neat but hesitant script. That was all. But that was enough. Enough to make Sophia ecstatic and sorrowful at the same time. Not only was Matthew not a Muslim, he was also not of her own time. Supposing that he miraculously asked her to marry him, and then she were suddenly transported back to her own time? What would she do then? And what would *he* do? She suddenly felt like a con artist—like she was fooling these people into thinking she was something she was not. The truth of her circumstances and her real history weighed far more heavily upon her at that moment than it had at any time since she had arrived.

Abby asked her if she was ready to blow out the lamp, and she absentmindedly did so, but her thoughts were complicated and jumbled. She remembered that next week would be her birthday. If she were home, she'd finally be getting her drivers' permit. As it was, she'd probably be snapping beans and helping the Sampsons put the windows in the new house. But after that, then what? Would she spend the rest of her life doing things like that, and never get to drive a car? Would she mind if she had to? When she'd first arrived, she hadn't been able to think of anything worse. Now she was beginning to fear being transferred back to her own time as much as she feared being stuck in 1857. She recited her prayers, but her eyes wouldn't close for a long time. At last her brain could think no more and she drifted off to sleep. She dreamed of driving her mom's car to the Sampsons new house and cooking peas in the microwave.

THE NEXT WEEK TURNED out to be so busy for Sophia that she didn't have much time to think of the heavy questions that had plagued her the night she received her journal from Matthew. She did try to write in it as often as possible, but never longer than a paragraph or so; she wanted to conserve precious space.

Sophia and Abby did help Mr. Sampson install the doorknobs and windows in the new house, and they also shelled MORE peas, and snapped beans and dug up the first potatoes. Summer was a busy time on the prairie, because so much had to be done in preparation for the next winter. Mrs. Sampson made pickled cucumbers with the salt Mr. Sampson had brought from town, and she also pickled some eggs and turnips. Mr. Sampson bought a piglet from a neighbor. He apologized to Sophia, but said that they needed the pork for next winter. Joshua named her Daisy, and he and Mr. Sampson set her up a pen behind the stable. Mrs. Sampson lent Sophia some metal hairpins so she could wrap her braid up after her hairband finally fell apart, and in return Sophia gave her a couple of the safety pins from her backpack. Mrs. Sampson used them for everything from pinning her apron down to holding her embroidery needles. Sophia wished she'd brought a whole package of them.

The house was coming along nicely—Mr. Sampson had most of the painting done. Mr. Edigar and Mr. Duncan were going to tend the Sampsons' wheat fields for the day or so it would take them to move into the new house, once it was finally ready. Sophia wondered how he was paying them. She knew there had to be some kind of barter; that's how things worked on the prairie.

One afternoon right after lunch, Mrs. Sampson saddled up Othello for Sophia and taught her the basics of riding. She said some women still rode side-saddle but even in her skirt, Sophia could not imagine such a thing. Mrs. Sampson laughed and said that when she had first come out, she had been appalled at women riding straddle-legged, but that now she also rode that way. She also confided, as if it were a great, embarrassing secret, that when she helped Mr. Sampson dig the well, or when she had to ride out and work in the fields, she wore a pair of her husband's trousers. Sophia said, "Well, it only makes sense! Sense is more valuable than manners, sometimes."

Mrs. Sampson seemed relieved. She laughed out loud. Then Abby saddled up Ophelia and Mrs. Sampson gave them a pail with lunch in it to take out to Mr. Sampson in the fields. As they set out, Abby helped Sophia get the feel of controlling the horse. Teaching seemed to do her good, and she spoke more confidently than Sophia had heard her speak since her arrival.

Sophia fell beautifully into riding, sitting comfortable and relaxed in the saddle, but she was somewhat timid about making the horse mind. Othello was well-trained, but he was a stallion, after all, and needed to know that his rider was confident and in control. He did what she commanded with her reins and feet until they got to the very edge of what was considered the soddy's yard. Beyond that, where the prairie grass grew tall and wasn't worn down, he refused to go. Sophia was afraid to smack him with the riding whip, because she was afraid she'd hurt him—*and* she was afraid he'd break into a gallop if she did. She could just imagine herself being dragged across the prairie by one foot caught in the stirrup! But Abby assured her he wouldn't run, and that if she ever wanted to ride she'd have to "make him mind." She explained that the whip was a tool for telling the horse what she wanted, and that he expected that little smack. He was testing her. So she whacked him and kicked at the same time, telling herself as well as him, "Come on. I'm the boss." Amazingly, when she sounded and felt like she meant it, Othello snorted and started out across the prairie.

"See? He'll respect you now. Never let him get his way. He has to mind," Abby said.

Sophia was filled to overflowing with a sense of pride. This was more difficult and more fulfilling than driving a car! When Sophia's dad had taken her to practice driving, she had felt like she was mastering the new skill, but she never felt triumphant or proud, like this. She patted Othello's neck. She wanted to tell Abby about the comparison to driving. But, as with so many things, she had to cut off her words. She wrote about it that night in her journal instead.

The girls found Mr. Sampson inspecting his full wheat, which was such a good crop that the stalks bent a bit under the weight of their loads. They delivered his lunch to him and he showed them a couple of full shoots.

On the way back, Abby told Sophia that she was going to get out her knitting that evening. "It's getting time to start knitting things for the winter."

"Do you know how to crochet?" Sophia asked her.

"Yes, but I like knitting better. I like the click of the needles. When I was a little girl Ma used to sit in her rocker by the fireplace in my bedroom while she sang me to sleep, back in Boston. I would listen to her voice and her needles, and then wake up the next morning."

Sophia saw an opportunity to give Abby another teaching role. "I can crochet, but I never learned to knit," she told her. "Would you teach me?"

Abby didn't look at Sophia. "I taught someone else to knit last year. She died."

"Oh, Abby. I'm so sorry." Sophia didn't want her to know that she already knew about her past sorrows. She let Abigail tell the story.

"She was my sister, Olivia. She wanted to make a pair of mittens, but I told her she had to start out with a scarf, and when she knew how to knit well enough, then she could make mittens." Abby paused. "She never got to make them."

"What happened?" Sophia didn't know if she should ask or not, but it seemed that talking about it would be better for Abby than keeping it all bottled up like that.

"She got the smallpox. She was fine, Sophia. She was just fine. She was happy and strong and smart. And then when Ma came back from the Indian village last winter after she helped them through the pox, Livi caught them from her. She got a backache one day, and then a fever, and then a few days later the rash came. It was awful. She was all oozy and swollen, and she kept saying it burned. Then the pox turned blue and she stopped saying anything that made sense. And she started to smell. It was like she was decaying already, but she was still alive. Then she just went to sleep and never woke up. Ma saved Adoeet, but she couldn't save Olivia." Abby didn't cry, but she stared straight ahead.

"Oh, Abby! I am so sorry. I can't imagine how hard it must have been for you." *Or how much guilt Mrs. Sampson must carry with her*, she thought.

"My best friend Margaret died last year, too."

"In my religion, when someone dies we say, '*Inna li lahi wa inna alaihi rajaun.*' It means, 'From God we come, and to Him we return.'"

Abby didn't reply for a moment. Then she ventured, "Sophia. . .what does your religion say about why children are allowed to die?"

Sophia gulped. She wasn't prepared for a question like this. She knew that the younger girl's spirituality was being tested strongly, and she didn't want to turn her away from God with some lame response. So she thought a minute before she spoke.

"Well, Abby, we believe that the purpose of this life is to get to the hereafter. Like this life is just the journey and the end of the journey is either heaven or hell. Of course we all strive for heaven, and ask God to forgive our sins so that we can get there. When small children die, we believe that they do not have to answer for any sins on the Day of Judgment. They just get to go straight to heaven. But we also believe that they can be like shepherds for their parents and families. That God blesses their families with heaven if they are patient through the pain and sorrow of a child's death. And then when the family members die, the little child takes them by the hand and leads them to heaven."

Sophia waited on edge to see how her words would be accepted. She looked over to find Abby staring straight at her.

"We also believe everything that happens to us is by the will of God," she went on, "and that He uses the events in our life to help us shape and grow our faith. We become stronger, wiser, more patient, and more blessed when we suffer hardship. And also. . ." Sophia wasn't sure if she should add the rest. "Also, we believe that sometimes things happen that we think at first are bad, but they turn out to be protections for us. Like someone might miss a plane—train!—and then it crashes. God was saving you from being in the crash. If someone dies young, maybe they would have experienced something so difficult in later life that they would lose their faith. So He is protecting them from that."

Abby was silent as she seemed to be mulling those things over. After a few minutes, she said thoughtfully, "That makes sense."

"You want to hear a story about that?" asked Sophia, more to break the silence than anything else.

"Alright" answered Abby.

"When Prophet Moses, upon him be peace, was

rather young, he met a great spiritual wise man. He asked the wise man to teach him all that he knew, and let him travel with him. The man agreed but told Moses that he could not ask any questions during the trip. Prophet Moses agreed, and off they went.

"They were walking by the sea, and they soon came to a small boat. They asked for passage across and the people agreed to take them across for a very small price. Shortly after the ship set sail, the wise man cut a hole in the bottom of it. It started to leak and the people had to bail out water at a furious pace to keep it afloat long enough to get back to shore."

"Why on earth did he do *that*?" asked Abby, incredulous. "That's exactly what Prophet Moses asked. But the man said, 'Remember, we had an agreement!' and so Prophet Moses kept quiet.

"Then they came to a small village. They saw a young boy playing in the street with some other children. When he was alone, the wise man killed him."

"Oh, my lands!"

"Yes! Can you imagine? Of course Prophet Moses had to ask what THAT was all about. 'That boy was completely innocent!' he said. 'Why did you kill him?' 'Remember our pact,' was the man's reply. So Prophet Moses very unhappily kept quiet again."

The girls had reached the stable by now, and

began unsaddling the horses.

"Then they came to another village where the people were really mean. They wouldn't give them food or water or shelter for the night. On the way out of the town, the wise man saw a broken old wall. He toiled for a couple of hours, rebuilding it, and then just started walking away.

"Well, this was it for Moses. He said, 'OK, I remember our agreement. But I can't stand this anymore. Please tell me why you did all those things. And why don't you at least go ask the people of this city for some payment for fixing their wall? We could get food and shelter for the night!' So the man said, 'You don't have enough patience to study with me. I will tell you the reasons for all those things, but then we must part company.'

"Prophet Moses agreed and the man said, 'God instructed me to do those things.' Moses looked doubtful. 'The people who owned the boat were kind and good, but poor. Taking people across the sea in that boat was the only way they had to make a living. But a nasty king was out and about on the water that day. He was stealing ships from everyone to put in his navy fleet. When he came to the boat of our friends, he saw it had a hole, so he left it with them. The hole was easy to repair, and it saved their boat from being stolen.'

"'Aaahhhhhh,' said Prophet Moses.

"'The young man I killed was the child of good, kind, faithful parents. He was not beautiful and kind, though, and was going to grow up into a nasty person who would test his parents' faith and cause them to turn away from God. But being patient when a child dies is one of the ways that God, through His grace, grants people paradise. Now the boy's parents will be granted Paradise instead of hellfire on account of him, and Allah will bless them with a better son in his place.

"'And the wall I just rebuilt belonged to a man who died recently. He left underneath it a treasure for his two young orphaned sons. If the wall had fallen, the greedy people of the town would have taken the boys' treasure.'

"So Prophet Moses had to leave the man's company, but he had learned his lesson. That everything God does has a reason and we have to have faith that things will always work out for the best, even when we can't see the good in things."

Abby put her saddle on the wooden stable horse and looked at Sophia. "I can't believe that Olivia was going to be a nasty person."

"Oh, of course not. It's not like that's the only reason children die. Not at all. But the point is that there are things that God knows that we don't know. And He asks us to trust Him and believe that He is the Best of Planners."

"That makes sense," Abby said again. And she turned and walked toward the house.

THE NEXT AFTERNOON ABBY and Sophia cleaned up the lunch dishes and then set about washing the candle mold so they could make new candles as soon as the evening cooled off a bit. Abby complained to Sophia that she dreaded doing this chore in the summer. It entailed boiling animal fat they had saved in an iron pot in the small shed and then pouring the boiling fat into molds. After the candles cooled awhile, they had to dip them in boiling water for a moment so they would slip easily out of their molds. Sophia knew it would be hot work, but she was looking forward to it. A lady from the conservation department had come to her school once and taught them how to make candles and it had been really fun. They'd dipped their fingers in the warm wax and peeled it off. Thoughts of home were becoming more like soft memories now, not as sharp and painful as they had been when Sophia first arrived.

As they were washing the candle molds in a bucket on the table, there was a light knock on the open door. When Sophia looked up, she was shocked to see an elderly black man standing in the doorway, floppy old felt hat in hand.

"Oh, good afternoon, Mr. William!" exclaimed Mrs. Sampson. "It's so nice to see you. Please come in."

The old man ducked his head just a bit so he'd fit through the doorway and stepped inside.

"How are things with you?" asked Mrs. Sampson.

"Aaww, jes fine, Ma'am. How's your family?"

"Doing well, thank you, Mr. William. You haven't met Sophia. She's from New York and is staying with us."

"How'do, Miss," said Mr. William, inclining his head. The old man had close-cropped, curly gray hair and a beard that still had a little bit of black in it. He had obviously been a very large man at one time, but now he was rather stooped. He wore an old gunnysack with a head hole and arm holes cut out of it and a small length of rope around the waist. His trousers were faded and thin, patched many times. Like everyone else on the prairie in late June, he was barefoot. He was missing a couple of teeth, but that didn't change the kindness of his smile.

"I'm fine, thank you. Nice to meet you."

"Mrs. Sampson, the massa sent me over to ask

if we could borrow your post hole digger. We's fixin' to make a corral. Massa's mare just birthed a little foal."

MASSA?

"Awww. I hope it went well. Certainly, you can borrow it. It's in the stable. And here, take some of this stew over to Miss Evaline."

"Thank you kindly, Ma'am. She'll surely appreciate it. Massa also wanted me to tell you he's going to town next week if ya'll need anythin'." The man spoke English easily, but had a slight accent. Something that sounded lilting and familiar to Sophia.

"We're fine, actually. Mr. Sampson just went to town recently. Would you like to sit down and relax a bit?"

"Oh, no, thank you, Ma'am. I got to git back and start diggin' those fence posts." He nodded at Sophia, "Welcome to the territory, Miss."

"Thank you, Mr. William," Sophia managed. But she was so dumbstruck by what she had just heard that she had to force herself to look away from him, for fear she was staring rudely.

When he had gotten the fence post digger and was gone, walking slowly across the plains alone—no horse, no nothing—Sophia looked open-mouthed at Mrs. Sampson, who nodded sadly. Sophia still had to ask out loud. "Is he. . .a slave?"

"Yes, dear."

"Oh, my God. How? I thought slaves were only in the south?"

"They decided awhile back that those of us here in the Kansas and Nebraska territories should be able to decide whether to be slave territories or free. Of course if we had just been able to decide for ourselves, we would have chosen to be free territories. But the southern states sent people here by the hundreds. Some to settle and some just to vote. They managed to get the original vote passed as a slave territory and now there are a lot of difficulties; lots of fighting between the two camps. Border Ruffians are always coming over from Missouri and attacking abolitionists. They are so vile. Can you imagine killing people because they believe in freedom for everyone? It's so unChristian-like."

"Who does Mr. William. . .'belong' to?"

The answer hit Sophia like a dagger. "The Jordans. Like the others, they came here for one reason and one reason only: to ensure that Kansas becomes a slave state. I don't know how they sleep at night. They know that we are all serious settlers, who came here to live and who don't own or approve of owning slaves. But they still act like they are perfectly normal homesteaders—keeping up this façade of being neighborly, even though everyone knows about their slaves and their real reason for being here."

So that's what Mrs. Jordan had meant by all that

vulture talk. She wanted to make sure that slavery was extended into the new territories, so that the "Southern way of life" could triumph and continue. Sophia thought frantically. . .when had the Civil War begun? She couldn't remember when it started but she remembered from 9th grade history that it had ended in 1865. Her head reeled. How could she have missed the historic significance of the time in which she'd arrived? She had been deposited right into the middle of Bleeding Kansas: this place was as violent now as most places were during the Civil War itself. No wonder everyone carried guns!

Sophia sank weakly to the table. She looked from Abby to Mrs. Sampson and thought about Mr. William. He seemed so kind and. . .it was so unfair. Sophia knew that slavery had existed, of course, but she was still reeling at being actually confronted with it. Her emotions swarmed inside her. Anger, hatred, pity, frustration, bewilderment. How could that nice Mrs. Jordan be a slave owner?

"Why didn't you tell me?"

Mrs. Sampson considered her answer. "Well, I'm a bit embarrassed to admit it. When you first arrived, we considered the possibility that you might be. . .a spy or a plant from Missouri or another slave state. But you seemed so disoriented and you don't have a southern accent and. . .well. . .we prayed on it and decided you weren't." This revelation would normally have shocked Sophia, but she was already in such a state of disbelief that it barely registered.

"Is he the only slave they have?" she asked.

"No," answered Mrs. Sampson. "They also have a nurse for Samuel. Miss Evaline. She practically raises him while Mrs. Jordan does her hair and attends formal dinners."

"Are they the only ones? How about the Duncans, the Edigars. . .everyone else?"

"The Edigars are fence sitters. They don't own slaves, but they don't mind if other people do. The Duncans are abolitionists like us, although Mrs. Duncan is more active in the cause than I am, bless her heart. I haven't had the heart to do much since. . ." She looked at Abby. "Well, since last winter. Most of the rest of the neighbors are like us, although some of the folks around here are called Free-Soilers or Free Staters. That doesn't mean they believe in freedom for Negroes. They just want Kansas to be all white, because they don't want Negroes—slave or free—to take away jobs from the white men. They also don't want the plantation system to be imported here, because it would drive regular homesteaders out. So they are technically aligned with us, but they are spiritually and philosophically a world apart. Thank goodness none of our neighbors is like that. We had a great Governor, Governor Geary, but this new President, Buchanan, is pro-slavery. Governor Geary resigned in March."

"But Mrs. Jordan seemed so nice," Sophia protested faintly, her hands still shaking.

"I know, it's strange. It's like some people have a blind spot where slavery is concerned. They are kind and giving to other people, but they just don't see slaves as people. They see Negros -- and Indians, too, for that matter -- as inferior creatures. They let themselves become blind to God's word and God's mercy. And then their hearts decay. It makes their kindness to whites seem like poison."

Sophia stared at her. She could not process what she had just learned. She went outside and looked at the back of the kind black man, almost out of sight across the grass. Suddenly she didn't want to make candles anymore.

THAT NIGHT SOPHIA FOUND herself lying awake again, long after she had blown out the lamp. She got up from the mattress and slipped out into the night. The weather had been getting hotter, but the night air was cool and calm, and belied all that she felt inside. She was still amazed every time she saw the stars here, and in the middle of the night they were even more brilliant than they were just before the dawn prayer, when she usually saw them. She walked a little ways from the house, watched the stars blur, and gave herself over to hot, furious tears. She cried for herself—for her loneliness and her lack of purpose or meaning here. She cried for her family—for her mom who should have been taking her to get her permit but who might be crying her own eyes out for all Sophia knew. She cried for Adoeet—for the senseless humiliation he had to endure at the hands of the children whose parents and grandparents had ripped apart his entire culture. But she cried mostly for Mr. William. A dear old man who she assumed had spent his entire life as a prisoner—a piece of property—and whose only crime was to have been born black. She cried because she was angry and because she was lonely and because she was confused. How could she have carried on so blithely when she was back home, naively reaping the benefits of living in a country that was created on the backs of people like Adoeet and Mr. William? As she cried, she cursed everyone who was prejudiced against anyone, anywhere, at any time, for any reason. She cried until her head ached. Then she cried because there wasn't even something as simple as a Kleenex to comfort her.

After awhile she heard someone behind her. She sniffed as she turned her head and found Abby, in her own night dress. She didn't say anything or ask any questions, she just sat beside Sophia and let her cry until she had no more in her. "It's so unfair, Abby," she finally managed to say. "How dare they think they own him!" she said when she had gotten control of her voice again.

"What does your religion say about things like that?"

"Well. . ." She thought awhile. "In the old days, people used to have slaves. But not like this. Not slaves because of their color. Slaves were prisoners of war or things like that. Slaves were just a part of the world before Islam came. But Islam taught people to house and feed their slaves in exactly the same manner they did themselves, and people were always encouraged to free slaves. Slaves could marry free people, and if a child was born to slave woman and her master, both the mother and the child were free. Slaves could also earn enough money to buy their freedom. So the whole institution of slavery was slowly abolished.

"I meant what does your religion say to do when you see evil being committed?"

Sophia blinked. "Well, it says to correct it with your hand if you can, or with your words if you can, or at least hate it in your heart."

"My heart is tired of hating it. I want to correct it."

Sophia was stunned.

"Yeah," she agreed. "We should arrange for them to run away. That'd serve those Jordans right!" Then her excitement dampened a bit. "But even if we somehow freed them, the problem would still exist. There would still be other slaves."

"Yes, but Sophia, at least we would have helped the people we know. I love Mr. William. He sneaked out to come to Olivia's funeral. The Jordans don't come to the Methodist services because half the time the sermons are about abolishing slavery. And their slaves are *certainly* not allowed to come. But Mr. William risked punishment to come say goodbye to Livi."

Sophia stared at Abby. This was a side of her that Sophia hadn't even suspected existed. Whereas Sophia's first impressions of her were of a timid, even delicate young girl, her eyes shone now with earnest determination. She was showing the strength and fortitude that her hardships had bred in her.

"You know what, Abby? You're right. Let's do it. Do you think we could actually free them, or help them escape?"

"I think we have to try. I'm tired of sitting around hating slavery, but doing nothing about it. Until Livi died, my parents used to go to abolitionist meetings, and my ma even wrote some of the pamphlets they pass around in Westport. So at least we were doing something. Now. . .well. . .there is a lady in Kansas Town named Susan Coate. She's a famous abolitionist and Mrs. Duncan knows her from the meetings she goes to. Maybe she could help us."

"OK. Let's get to bed now. We can plan in the morning while we milk the cows."

"Good idea." Abby hugged her. A shocked Sophia hugged her back, her self-pity and frustration forgotten. Then they went in and slept like babies.

The next morning, Abby and Sophia milked the cows in record time. All the while, they discussed how they could get Mr. William and Miss Evaline away from the Jordans. They imagined scenarios as crazy as riding to the Jordan place and saying their house was on fire and they needed Mr. William to come help put it out. What about Miss Evaline, though? While they were weeding the garden and gathering lettuce they came up with lots of other ideas, but they seemed just as far-fetched. They decided to talk to Mrs. Duncan and try to talk to Mrs. Coates if they could. Abby said she might be at the Fourth of July celebration that was coming up the next week.

That afternoon Jacques came over in his wagon.

"I was delivering a load of firewood to old Mrs. Wilson," he told Mrs. Sampson as he drank the cold, fresh well water she'd offered him. "She says that the Reece boys are lookin' fer someone ta watch over that girl of theirs while they're harvestin'. I thought maybe young Sophia here might be interested in the job."

Babysitting? Sophia involuntarily wrinkled up her nose. She was no good with small children. She had never offered to babysit for ladies in the community, like her friends did. She didn't even care that they made money doing it. She hoped Mrs. Sampson would say she needed her here at home.

No such luck.

"Why, Jacques, that sounds like a wonderful idea," Mrs. Sampson gushed.

"Stan Reece is a dern good roofer. Maybe he can put the roof on yer new place for ya as payment." He handed Mrs. Sampson the tin dipper from the well and got back up into his wagon.

"Yes, that might work. Thank you for the message, Jacques. We'll talk it over with Joseph when he gets in this evening."

Sophia was dying. She knew that if the Sampsons wanted her to babysit for the Reeces, she'd do it without complaining. They had done so much for her, how could she refuse? But she also knew she'd hate every single second of it.

Mrs. Sampson saved her from her terror.

"Clara Reece would be very easy for you to care for, Sophia. As a young child. . .oh, probably a bit smaller than Joshua. . .she was kidnapped by Indians. She was raised by them most of her life. Of course all the time she was gone her family was desperate to find her, and her ma died a couple of years ago from sheer heartbreak. But her pa and her brother kept looking for her, and they were finally able to locate her, with the help of an Indian guide. Earlier this spring, after a surprise ice storm, they rescued her. Of course, she's a lot older now. She'd been gone almost ten years. She's a young woman now. The Reeces were so excited to have her back, but her leg and a couple of her ribs were broken during the rescue, and she's still not well.

Apparently she doesn't speak English anymore. The trauma of her kidnapping may have damaged her mind as well—that's not uncommon. She's been home maybe three months now, but still hasn't spoken to anyone. She doesn't remember how to keep house or anything. Do you think you could keep her company and tend their little cabin?"

Sophia was so relieved that Clara Reece wasn't a toddler that she happily agreed. She wondered if she'd have to feed her and everything, or just sit with her. But even if she had to care for her in the most basic ways, she would be glad to help out. What a horrific way to grow up, kidnapped back and forth. No wonder she wasn't all there.

Mr. Sampson nodded when he heard of the potential exchange. He said that Stan Reece was indeed a fine roofer, and that he'd go talk with him and work out the details of the swap. He asked Sophia if she was sure she wouldn't mind taking care of Miss Reece.

"No, I'm glad I'll finally have a way to pitch in and help the family." She was surprised to realize that she was really thinking of the Sampsons as family now.

"Abby will go with you if you like. And we'll have to teach you to shoot before you go. Just in case," said Mr. Sampson.

Sophia looked at him. "In case what?"

"Well, in case of wolves or horse thieves or something. And there is a slight possibility that the Indians might come looking for her."

"Don't worry, dear." Mrs. Sampson's strong, comforting voice assured her as she patted Sophia's hand. "If the Indians really wanted her back, they would have come to get her already. I truly don't think you'll have any trouble. And the Reeces live near the river, so their house is pretty protected on that side. But closer to the river there is a higher chance of wild animals paying you a visit, so it really is a good idea to learn to handle a shotgun."

Sophia remembered watching *Bowling for Columbine* with her parents and cringed. But this was a whole different world. Here, guns weren't for recreation or power or criminal violence. They were just survival. She found herself looking forward to learning to shoot.

The next morning, Sophia and Abby didn't have time to even think about their plan to free the Jordans' slaves. Mrs. Sampson took them out shooting. Eleanor Sampson sure was full of surprises. She handled the long gun she'd retrieved from under her bed with practiced ease. She set an old tin target up on the side of the wagon and shot it down twice in a row. Joshua begged for a turn so she let him practice while she explained the use of the gun to Sophia.

"This is a Greener 12-gauge. It's a shotgun. A shotgun is easier to use than a rifle because it has many little balls of shot that spray out of it, covering a larger area. So you don't have to be an expert shot in order to hit your target. Rifles shoot only one bullet at a time, so they are more difficult to master."

Even Joshua was able to hit the target. Sophia took the gun from him when he offered it to her, and he got a kick out of her reaction. Two things surprised her: it was extremely heavy, and it was warm to the touch. The others had held it and shot it so easily that Sophia was shocked at how much it weighed. It felt unwieldy, but she quickly slapped on her casual face, not to be outdone by Joshua. She loaded it the way Mrs. Sampson showed her, and took her time aiming at the target.

Next thing she knew she was stumbling backward. She didn't even remember hearing the shot go off. She just felt the tremendous kick of the gun and staggered back, almost falling on her behind.

So much for casual!

Joshua cracked up. Even Abby covered her mouth and giggled as she helped Sophia steady herself. At least she hadn't fallen flat!

She reloaded and tried again. This time she was ready for the kick and she stood steady, but she still didn't hit the target. Mrs. Sampson had only brought three more rounds of ammunition. Sophia hit the target once, but the last time missed again. She wished they had more ammo, because she felt she was just starting to get the hang of it.

"We'll come out again tomorrow morning," said

Mrs. Sampson. "Your shoulder needs to get used to shooting and we really need to get home and put lunch on."

That night when Mr. Sampson came in, he told them that Sophia's work with the Reece family was all set up, and she'd start the next Monday, right after the Fourth of July. Mr. Sampson would take her over to their place every morning when he went out, and pick her up before he came home. Her days would be long, but she was getting excited about meeting Clara.

The next morning while she was milking the cows, Sophia thought her right arm would fall off at the shoulder. She had to take a folded towel with her to put against her shoulder when she shot that afternoon. It didn't seem to help much. That evening when she looked at her shoulder there was a big greenish bruise—but she had hit the target several times that afternoon. She was proud.

SOPHIA WAS AMAZED BY the Fourth of July celebration. Back home, they sometimes went to Hutchinson to spend the Fourth with her grandparents. Her Dad and Grandpa grilled the meat while the ladies made potato salad, pasta salad, Jell-O salad, and plain old salad salad. They always had corn on the cob, which the kids shucked, and homemade ice cream. Then they sat on the deck of Grandma's house and watched the fireworks at the nearby stadium. Between the picnic and the fireworks, they all played cards. It was a family affair with a relaxed, homey atmosphere.

Here, July Fourth was a huge celebration that involved the entire community. Sophia was excited because she would finally see "Kansas Town" itself. It had rained again a few days before the Fourth, and everyone was afraid it would be muddy for the festivities. Abby said there was no way to have fun while you were wading around in ankle-deep mud. They even talked of skipping the celebration if it didn't dry out, but the day before the holiday it was hot and sunny all day, and the ground dried almost completely.

They were going to celebrate in Westport, which was just one of several small towns in the area, and which by the time Sophia was born would be a quaint, historic shopping district. Sophia couldn't wait to see it.

The day before the trip, the girls made cornbread and fried chicken with Mrs. Sampson. They even used up the last bit of the white flour to make a plum pie. They made buttered green beans, and sliced up about ten cucumbers from the garden, mixing them with onions and vinegar. Then they packed everything in the big picnic basket that was kept in the root shed. They put the full basket back in the shed so it would stay cool, and turned in early.

The next day, Mrs. Sampson woke them well before sunrise. Sophia wondered how she got up so early without an alarm clock. They did all the chores and piled into the wagon to get started by mid-morning. Sophia had long since stopped wondering what time it actually was. She was the only Muslim she knew who could tell when it was time for the dawn prayer by the way the creatures started to rustle, the cock crowed, and the sky started to change its mood from solid and dark to tentatively gray over in the East, or who gauged the time for the afternoon prayer by seeing if the shadows were as long as their objects. She climbed into the wagon and settled down beside Joshua, who had his top, his pocketknife, and a homemade bow with him. Abby had brought her knitting, but she was too excited to knit on the way out. Sophia hadn't brought her journal, but she had sneaked a thank-you note for Matthew into the picnic basket. She had taken one of the pages out of the journal and composed a hundred notes in her head before she settled on one. She wanted something that expressed her gratitude without seeming too familiar or personal. "*Matthew, thank you for the journal. Your kindness is greatly appreciated*," is what she had finally settled on and tucked away in the basket, not knowing if it was wise to actually give it to him or not. She didn't want to be flirting, but on the other hand she had not had a chance to thank him at all. She didn't want him to think she was ungrateful or stuck up. In any case, the note was there. She would ask Mrs. Sampson to give it to him, if she had the courage.

Sophia looked at her bare feet. She felt embarrassed to go to a public event barefoot. Muslims wore stocking feet when they were in the mosque, but this was different. This would be outside. And Mrs. Sampson was wearing shoes for the first time since Sophia had arrived.

Sophia asked Abby about it. "Oh, those are her

'Back East' shoes. She only wears them when we go to town. But most people—even women—don't wear shoes in the summer at all. I don't even have shoes anymore. I outgrew mine by spring. We'll get a new pair in the fall when school starts. Grownups usually have boots, but they're only for working or when it snows. If you wear them in the summer, you just waste shoe leather." Sophia grinned to herself. Her grandpa always used that expression. Now she knew where it came from.

So Sophia relaxed a bit. Still, though, she hoped she wouldn't stick out like a sore. . .toe!

The ride to town was exactly like a family car ride back home, except bumpier. Josh kept trying to spin his top on the wagon bed but the uneven trail made it bounce and land on its side. The girls chatted, and Mr. and Mrs. Sampson sat up on the wagon seat. Sadie even stuck her head over the side of the wagonbed, just like dogs back home stuck their heads out car windows. They saw the Duncans and the Edigars on the way, and Mrs. Sampson pointed out different peoples' homes, including Matthew's. It sported a large vegetable garden with straight rows and a very well-made scarecrow. Sophia's overall impression was that it was extremely neat for being a bachelor cabin.

The town looked exactly like pictures of old towns that Sophia had seen in books, except it was splashed with color. The buildings weren't painted, so they weren't very different from the old pictures, but the people were bright and their clothes were like an artist's pallet. The ladies were dressed in everything from old, faded gingham dresses with ties around the waists to tightly cinched dresses with corsets and bustles and fancy hats. Some women wore hoop skirts and looked so quaint sitting on the ground with the hoops spread out all around them. Sophia wondered how they managed to do anything in those clumsy-looking things. And Abby had been right; all of the younger people and many of the women were indeed barefoot, even some of the ones who were dressed up.

On one side of the main street were shops with a wooden sidewalk in front of them. There was "Johnson's General Store" and "Westport Wagon Supplies." On one corner there was a blacksmith's shop, but no blacksmith today. All the stores except the general store were closed, their owners enjoying the holiday. On the other side of the street was a large meadow with an three-sided barn-like structure that Mrs. Sampson said was the place where city officials gave speeches and where the debating society met and things like that.

The weirdest thing about Westport, though, was that it seemed to have multiple personalities. Most of the people were hardworking, regular families, laughing with their kids and their neighbors and having a pleasant afternoon. The men were playing ball and running races—some were even playing music on harmonicas and fiddles—and children were dashing around everywhere. The women were busy getting food out or working on needlework while chatting with each other. But there were also a good many drunks wandering around the place. Abby said around the corner there were saloons, and that's where they were getting topped off. These men were actually unsteady on their feet, and went around talking loudly and trying to join the ballgames. Sophia also saw two Indians among this group. They wore Indian style hair and moccasins, and one had on chaps with leather fringe on the sides of his legs. But they wore frontier-style shirts and the other one actually had on overalls like Jacques'. The scary part, though, was that all the drunks carried guns, just like the other men. Sophia had never seen a drunk person. Their behavior was humiliating, and she was glad that alcohol was forbidden in Islam. She hoped none of them would cause any trouble.

The third group of people who made up the crowd that day in Westport were the African Americans. There were only a few, and they were dressed shabbily. Sophia noticed two groups that looked like families, but most of the rest were slaves of the white people. Their eyes were drawn, even when they were smiling, and when Sophia compared them to the faces of the homesteaders she saw the weight of oppression. White people had hard lives here, too. They worked hard, many died young, most had lost family members. . .but they were free, and that made their faces light.

Mrs. Sampson caught her surveying the crowd. "I can't believe those people have the audacity to bring their slaves here. I hope there won't be any trouble," she said, her eyes sweeping over the crowd.

"Me, too," agreed Sophia. Then she caught Abby's eye. "Let's go see Mrs. Duncan."

The girls found Emma Duncan near her wagon, unloading her family's basket. Adoeet was already sitting on his blanket and the rest of her kids were off playing with the others. The small ones were nearby and occasionally came running to her with small needs or complaints.

"Good morning, Mrs. Duncan," said Abby as they walked up.

"Oh, mornin', girls. How're you enjoying the Fourth?"

"It's wonderful," said Sophia.

"I just love these picnics. I don't get to see my Henry have fun very often. I like to see him let go of all his worries."

Sophia knew that she meant the worries of farming and homesteading as well as the worries of being an active abolitionist in a territory torn apart over the issue.

"Mrs. Duncan, can we ask you something?"

"Why, sure, Abigail. What do you need, dear?"

"Well, it's kind of serious."

Mrs. Duncan put down her basket. "Oh, well, then, sit here with me." She indicated the blanket and the three sat down.

Abby began, "Mrs. Duncan, we were thinking. We hate to see Mr. William and Miss Evaline living like that over at the Jordans. Do you think there's any way your Abolitionist Society could help us help them escape?" She looked around and then whispered, "We want to free them."

Sophia nodded her agreement.

"Oh, girls!" Mrs. Duncan exclaimed, and then lowered her voice. "You two are such good girls, bless your hearts. But actually, we've talked to Mr. William several times, and he doesn't want to risk trying to escape."

The girls looked at each other. This was something they hadn't anticipated.

"Well, it's not that he likes being a slave. Of course not. But he's old, girls. His family has already been sold away from him, and he doesn't know anything else in life except working on a farm. If he were free, he'd have to find a place to live, start earning money. . .do it all himself, probably. And all that would be AFTER he managed to survive the trip; he'd have to make it at least past Iowa, which would be difficult on someone his age. He doesn't feel like he could make it through all that at this late stage in his life. So all we can do for him—and Evaline—is to support them by being kind to them, and by trying to change the laws so that when Kansas does enter the union, we will be a free state."

"But how do we do that?" Abby was as frustrated as Sophia.

"And even if we did that, it still won't help Mr. William. Can't he come live with you, or us, or someone?"

"Abby, honey, it's not legal to free a slave unless you're the owner." There was that word again. "And I wouldn't mind breaking that particular law, but if we freed Mr. William and then took him to one of our houses, the Jordans would be within their legal rights to take him back. In fact, according to the Fugitive Slave Act, anyone who knew where he was would be obligated to return him to them. And then his life would really be difficult."

The girls were deflated; all the fun seemed to have been drained out of the day. Who knew that freedom could be trumped by practical considerations? All Sophia and Abby wanted was help Mr. William. And it seemed that the obstacles to doing that were not just the Jordans—not just the institution of slavery—but also Mr. William himself and all the logistical difficulties freedom posed for him.

"I'm sorry, ladies. I know it's frustrating when you want to help so badly. And Abby, I know your parents are strong abolitionists, too. I remember your mother's enthusiasm and hard work for the cause back before. . .Olivia's smallpox." Mrs. Duncan changed the subject quickly. "I hear you two are taking care of Miss Clara Reece, though. That's certainly a good deed," she offered. "She was taken by a band of Kiowa. That's Adoeet's tribe, but it was a band from somewhere out West in the territory that took her. Apparently she later wound up with another tribe altogether. That's one reason that it was so hard for the Reeces to find her. Thank God our local bands don't usually go in for kidnapping. The Kiowa are a proud, warring tribe, but we've tried very hard to build a good relationship with them here. I've never heard of them kidnapping anyone." She sighed. "I hope she starts readjusting soon. Perhaps having you there will open her up a bit, Sophia. I hope she's not been so traumatized that she will never be right in the head again. . ."

"Me, too," said Sophia, but she was really still thinking about Mr. William. She could see Mrs. Jordan from where she sat, and she prayed that the Southern woman wouldn't try to talk to her. Sophia wasn't sure she could be responsible for what she might say to that arrogant, ignorant beast of a woman.

The girls helped Mrs. Duncan keep an eye on her smaller children for a while, then headed back over to their own blanket. They watched some younger girls play a game called "Graces." They tossed wooden rings back and forth, catching them on wooden wands. It didn't look too exciting to Sophia, and the sun was just past straight overhead, so she made her way over to the brand new public pump across the street on the corner by the blacksmith's shop, and made her ablutions. It was hot and the water from the pump felt wonderful as she washed her face, arms and feet, but it couldn't rinse away the bitterness she still felt about not being able to help Mr. William. She made her way across the street behind the Sampsons' wagon to pray her mid-day prayer.

As she bent over and touched her head to the ground, Sophia heard someone near her. She hoped it wasn't one of those obnoxious children who had made fun of Adoeet, or some stranger wondering what she was doing back there.

When she finished her prayer, Sophia glanced to her left, where the sounds had come from.

There, standing very close to her and looking as if he'd seen a ghost, was Mr. William.

"Why, hello, Mr. William," Sophia began. "I was just praying."

"I know," he said, and paused. "*As Salaamu Alaikum.*"

Sophia looked back at him with her mouth half open. She didn't even answer him for a moment, she was so stunned.

"*Wa Alaikum asSalaam,*" she finally managed.

"Are you. . .a Muslim?" As Sophia heard his voice, she realized why his accent had sounded familiar. He was obviously a slave who had come over directly from Africa! She could still hear the faint accent of his homeland, and it had reminded her of the voices of her Somali and Sudanese friends back home.

"Yes."

"*SubhanAllah*!" he exclaimed in Arabic. Praise God! Then he glanced around guiltily.

Sophia, puzzled, looked furtively around, too, but didn't see anyone near them.

"Mr. William. . .*SubhanAllah*! Where are you from?"

"I'm a Mandinka, Miss Sophia. I grew up on the banks of the Gambia River."

"*Ya Allah! Tehki Arabi?*" she asked him. "Do you speak Arabic?"

"It's been a long time, Miss Sophia," he answered in English. "My Arabic is very bad, almost forgotten. But I can still recite Qur'an."

"Are there any other Muslims around here?" Sophia asked. She suddenly imagined an underground community of Muslims she could meet up with; hidden, but strong and unified. Her head was spinning with the joy of the idea.

"Oh, my lands, no," Mr. William disappointed her. "I's been in the new world goin' on forty years, now, and I never seen another Muslim, 'ceptin' other slaves. And even they've all been converted or sold away by now. Practicin' the faith is illegal for us, Miss Sophia. But you—where did you come from?"

Sophia gulped. She wanted to share her story, to spill out all of her bottled up history and stop carrying it around like a tumor in her chest. She knew she could trust this solid, quiet old man. But they were in a public place, where anyone could come upon them. It wasn't the right time, and it was too important to try and rush through.

"I'll tell you later, Mr. William. I can't tell you all of it now. It's a long story."

"Alright." He seemed to understand. He looked up over the top of the wagon and must have seen someone coming, because he dashed off quickly without even saying goodbye.

Sophia was still sitting on the ground after having finished her prayer. She got up slowly and brushed the grass off her skirts. *SubhanAllah*. Maybe there really was a reason she was here. As she walked around the wagon, she passed a young woman carrying a baby. She was obviously the reason Mr. William had hurried away so abruptly.

When she got back to the Sampsons' blanket, Mrs. Sampson was laying the food out. Sophia helped her. Soon the families started coming back in from their various activities and everyone began to eat. Abby was still sullen from their talk with Mrs. Duncan, but Sophia was excited now. She wished she could tell Abby what had happened, and vowed to do so—to tell her the whole story— as soon as they were alone.

Sophia was taking a drink of the cold pump water when she suddenly spotted Matthew sitting very near. He and Jacques were two blankets away, eating and chatting with another young man. Sophia thought of her note. She wondered how she could possibly have thought of such a thing. It was too forward and too embarrassing. When she glanced up again she found Matthew looking straight at her, smiling.

Sophia blushed; the corn cob she had been happily munching suddenly seemed very awkward and unladylike. She put it down and busied herself by going to refill her cup at the pump.

As she finished pumping the water, hoping that Matthew wasn't looking at her, she turned around to head back and ran smack into the last person she wanted to see. Rayetta Jordan stood right in her path. She didn't move. She looked at Sophia suspiciously, her warm southern bearing replaced by a business-like air.

"Mrs. Jordan. Excuse me. I didn't see you there."

"But apparently you did see my William."

Her William. Pleeeeaaaase.

"Jenny Dawson tells me she saw you two chatting in some foreign tongue, out behind the wagons."

Sophia didn't know what she felt more—panic or fury. "Oh, yes. Jenny Dawson probably heard me praying. I'm a Muslim and we don't pray in English, you know. And Mr. William did visit with me for a few minutes." Sophia put syrup into her voice. "That's OK, isn't it? I certainly didn't mean to offend you."

Mrs. Jordan was somewhat placated. "Well, I can't say as it's offensive, per se. We certainly allow our William to visit with people. Slaves are not pets, you know. But I do know that that family you stay with are abolitionist types. And while I can't imagine that you would be taken in by their naïve, misinformed mindset, I do have to protect my property. Mrs. Dawson felt very unsettled, seeing you talking with William behind the wagons. She said the two of you seemed unusually. . .engaged."

"Mr. William was just commenting on the beauty of my prayer, and how he liked the language. I was teaching him a few phrases. And I wish that if Mrs. . . ."

"Dawson."

"Yes, Mrs. Dawson. I've never even met her, by the way. I wish if she had wondered what was going on she would have spoken to me about it. I would have been happy to explain to her." Sophia was shocked at herself. She had never been so forthright with an adult. But this exchange was fueled by her fury.

"I see. Well, she probably wasn't comfortable talking to you with him present." Mrs. Jordan's shoulders relaxed and she reached out to touch Sophia's arm. It was all she could do to keep from pulling it away. "I'm glad we had this little talk.

William is a good worker and I'm glad you like him. In fact, you can borrow him any time you wish, if you can convince the Sampsons to accept his help. I know they don't like to accept slave labor, but really, laboring is what slaves enjoy. They like to be useful. If more Northerners understood that simple fact, there would be a lot less violence in this territory."

Sophia wanted to throw the cold water in Mrs. Jordan's face, but she didn't want to endanger her chances of seeing Mr. William in the future. She managed to reply with a smile, "Thank you for the offer Mrs. Jordan."

When she returned, she took Abby aside and told her a brief version of what had happened. Abby was shocked that Mrs. Jordan would have the gall to confront her in private like that. "Let's go tell Pa," she insisted. "He'll go give them what-for. He'll go talk to Mr. Jordan and lay down the law to him. My pa can be scary when he needs to be."

"No, let's wait," Sophia said. "Right now she thinks I might be on her side about slavery. She even offered to let me "borrow" William. That would be perfect because then we'd have time to talk with him and see if we can convince him to run away."

"Good idea. This way she'll be trying to win you over to her side, so she won't see anything coming."

The girls realized that the organized games and

contests were starting, so they joined the rest of the crowd on the side of the field and watched. The men ran foot races, played horseshoes, and had a shot-put style contest where they measured how far each man could throw an iron ball. (Sophia later learned they were cannonballs!) Mr. Sampson almost won the horseshoe contest, but a young boy who lived in the town rang one more shoe than he did. The girls laughed, because he was beaten not only by a young boy, but a tenderfoot city-boy at that!

Then came the main event: a wood-chopping contest. The festivities moved to the far side of the field where a pile of tree trunks had been set up. A man in a dusty old tuxedo rang a triangle—the kind they always ring for dinner in the movies. Then three men at a time stood at three tree stumps to chop as much wood as they could in five minutes. For a girl raised in the PlayStation age, this honest-to-goodness contest of real strength and endurance was more exciting than Sophia would have thought possible. She wished she could compete! The crowd cheered for their favorite contestants, and one of the drunks had to be removed for shouting obscenities. Sophia and Abby were laughing and talking with each other when the last group of three men took their places at the stumps. When the triangle rang, they looked up and Sophia was shocked to see Matthew at the middle stump. He had a bandana around his brow and store-bought leather gloves on his hands. The chops rang out and his pile grew larger and larger. When the triangle rang again, he had chopped more wood than his opponents. That meant he would advance to the next round.

Matthew and two other first-round winners rested while the other three winners battled it out. The victor was a mountain of a man. He must have been 6'5", and he chopped wood like John Henry drove railroad stakes!

When Matthew's group went back to the stumps, Sophia was amazed to see him win again, even though he'd had less rest than the other men. They were older gentlemen, though. Not as tough as the final round would be.

The man with the triangle let the men rest while another man took his bullhorn and began telling everyone about his amazing new stomach medicine, Hopstetter's Celebrated Stomach Bitters. It was hilarious. A pioneer infomercial.

When the crowd had had their fill of the stomach bitters and there were just a few poor suckers in line at Hopstetter's wagon, the referee again took up the bullhorn. Matthew and the Mountain Man took their places by the stumps for the final round of the chopping contest, and the referee rang the triangle yet again.

Sophia saw Matthew straining hard, bringing down his axe again and again. He concentrated so hard she knew he was probably unaware of the crowd or the noise or her. She remembered that this was how she had first seen him—chopping wood the evening Mr. Bodine had led her onto his property, still damp from the river and feeling like a drowned rat.

When the triangle rang again, indicating that the five minutes was up, Matthew stood back, took off his bandana and wiped his brow with it, just like he had done that first night. The ref counted the wood and announced to the cheering crowd that the other man, Jerry Janisson, had won the chopping contest. Matthew held out his hand and the two men shook heartily, slapping each other on the back as well. Sophia saw Matthew begin turning her way, in the process of raising his eyes to meet hers. She caught one split second of his blue eyes and nervously looked away. Not because she was embarrassed, really. She wanted so badly to congratulate him, and give him her note. . .but he was not for her. At least not unless she could find an appropriate way to explain her situation, get him to believe her, and then talk to him about Islam and convince him of its truth. . .but that was a pretty tall order, and who knew if he even liked her in a romantic way? Maybe he was just this kind and gallant to everyone. It broke her heart, but Sophia averted her gaze, and began chatting with Abby, who was waving at him. The girls turned and began walking back to the blanket.

When they returned, Mrs. Sampson was just

pulling the pie out of the picnic basket. Sophia had been excited about tasting it. She'd never made a pie from scratch before. It was sweetened with sorghum molasses, which was what the Sampsons used for every-day sweetening. Even Mr. Sampson's bitter coffee, which he drank only on Saturdays for some reason, was sweetened with the dull brown syrup. Sophia had gotten used to it, but she hadn't tasted any sweet other than cornbread or pancakes since she had arrived. She had often craved a Snickers bar, but this pie looked and smelled as good to her as any chocolate she'd ever had. She hoped it was, because only chocolate or something just as good could take her mind off the feelings she was developing for Matthew Collins.

Mr. Sampson came up out of the early evening, just as his wife began to serve the pie onto everyone's plates. Behind him were Jacques and Matthew.

"Brought us some good company to enjoy that pie of yours with, Eleanor," he said.

"Oh, hello Jacques, Matthew. Good to see you. Here you go." She scooped pieces of pie onto their plates, which they had brought with them. "Admirable job in the chopping contest, Matthew." Matthew sat on the blanket beside Abby. Sophia took a bite of her pie. It was every bit as sweet as she'd hoped. And the crust, made with their homemade butter and the last of the white flour, melted in her mouth.

"Thank you, Ma'am. Next year I'll get old Jerry."

"MMMmmm. Miz Eleanor, it's been a long time since I had a slice of actual pie. And I think this one must be about the best one I ever tasted," Jacques complimented her.

"Well, thank you, Jacques. The girls did most of the work, actually."

"Well, hats off to you, ladies," Matthew said, raising his fork in a polite salute.

Sophia peeked at him while he ate. His manners were polite but not stuffy, and he talked with Joshua in a friendly, comfortable way. So many other young men would either completely ignore a younger boy or treat him like a pest, but Matthew seemed genuinely interested in Josh's tales. He listened while Josh recounted his adventures at Edward's house, and even took a look at his bow. "That's a mighty fine job you've done there, Josh," he told him. "But the arrows need to be fletched or they'll never fly straight. I can show you how to do it if you like."

"Oh, yeah, Matt! That would be great!"

"Joshua!" scolded Mrs. Sampson. "You mean 'Oh, yes,' and 'thank you,' don't you?"

"Oh, yeah. I mean, yes. Thank you! That would be great. When can you come over and show me?"

"Well," Matthew inclined his head toward Mr. Sampson, "Let me talk to your pa."

"OK." Joshua finished his pie and asked if he could be excused to go play with Edward.

"Yes, dear, but make sure you stay close by. The fireworks will be starting soon," replied Mrs. Sampson.

Fireworks? Sophia hadn't realized they'd had fireworks in 1857. But shortly after they finished rinsing the plates at the pump, there they were. They were small—mostly a lot of noise and a few showers of sparks—but everyone oooohd and aaaaahd at them, just like they did back home for the huge, musical fireworks events Sophia remembered. The grand finale boasted red, white, and blue bursts, and everyone erupted into applause. At the close, they stood and sang a song that began "My Country, 'Tis of Thee," encouraged by a man with a bullhorn, and that was the end of the evening.

Some young people stayed for a dance that was being held in the street, to the tunes of fiddles, banjos and harmonicas, but the Sampsons didn't join them.

As Mrs. Sampson and the girls loaded everything back into the wagon, Mr. Sampson and Matthew hitched up the horses together. With a sudden rush of either courage or stupidity, Sophia sneaked her thank you note from the picnic basket and very casually asked Joshua to give it to Matthew. Then she made herself busy helping get everything ready to go, and didn't look in Matthew's direction again.

When the horses were hitched up and the blanket and basket settled into the back of the wagon, the Sampsons and Sophia piled in and set off. They waved to several families they passed, and said good night. Sophia was sad that the day was ending. Who knew how long it would be until they would have another day like that? She missed the sense of community that comes with doing things together with other people—even work. Living on the prairie was such a lonely affair. The Sampsons spent a lot more time together than modern families, which was usually nice, but the community was so spread out that the sense of common purpose and work she remembered from back home was lacking.

As soon as the Sampsons' wagon was out on the prairie alone and Sophia was just settling into the wagon bed, exhausted after all the festivities and the emotional ups and downs of the day, Mr. Sampson broke the family's silence.

"Miss Sophia, Matthew spoke with me about coming over later this week."

Sophia was perplexed. "Yes, he said he would."

"You knew?"

"Yes. He was telling Joshua he would try to come and teach him how to fix his arrows so they would fly straight."

Mr. Sampson laughed. "Well, he plans to help Josh with his arrows, but I think the arrows he's really interested in are Cupid's! He's asked my permission to come court you."

"Court me?" Sophia looked at Abby. It was after

dark but the prairie was dimly lit by the moon and stars. Sophia could barely make her out. She was furiously nodding her head. Sophia tried to appeal to Mrs. Sampson for help, but she was looking back from the wagon seat with a proud, motherly smile.

"Yep. Said he's been waitin' a long time for a young woman as down to earth as you. Said he wasn't ever taken by those giggly, kerchief-wavin' girls who are just out to catch a husband like men catch a fish. Said he'd almost given up and gone back home to let his ma find him a bride."

Sophia swallowed. She didn't know whether to jump for joy or jump off a cliff.

"He also said he was impressed by your gumption. He asked me about your religion, but I told him he'd have to talk to you about all that."

"My gumption?"

"Why, sure! You fell in a river and lost your whole family. But you still wake up every morning cheerful and brave, and he's impressed with the way you tackle things. Somehow you're able to just take what comes and make the best of it."

Sophia blinked in the near-darkness. She'd never heard herself described that way, nor considered herself a courageous person. Wouldn't Amani be shocked!

Mrs. Sampson agreed with her husband. "I've noticed that about you, too, Sophia. You're a strong young lady with strong faith. You lost your entire family and found yourself in a whole new life. And a difficult one, at that—living in a soddy and such. That kind of ordeal would have finished off most other city girls. But you just took up the burden and walked on. You're always helpful and have fit in wonderfully with our family. I should think Mr. Collins would be honored to be your husband. And he's not chased after everything in skirts, either, like some young men. He has indeed waited a good long while to begin courting. He must have been waiting just for you." To her husband she said, "Joseph, where is it he comes from?"

"Well, now. . .I'm not rightly sure. We can talk about all that durin' the courtin'."

Sophia didn't know what to say. Her cheeks were burning and she was glad that Joshua had already passed out beside her in the wagon bed.

"So whaddya say? Shall I invite him over?"

"Can I sleep on it?" Sophia asked.

"Surely. But don't make him wait too long. Poor boy's smitten like crazy." Mr. Sampson chuckled to himself and put his arm around his wife, scooting her closer to him on the wagon seat.

That Fourth of July was full of wonder for Sophia. She felt as if the fireworks were going off inside of her. Between finding out about Mr. William being a Muslim, having to confront Mrs. Jordan, and the courting proposal from Matthew, her head was spinning. She was looking forward to Monday when she'd be alone with Abby all day at the Reeces. She needed some time to pray and process all this.

Sunday was a relaxed day. Mr. Sampson went out to check on the wheat, which was almost ready for harvesting, but other than that they did only the most necessary chores. In the morning, after milking, the girls washed up all the dishes again (they had only been rinsed in town, under the pump) and returned the picnic basket to the shed.

While they were there, Sophia asked Abby what all courting entailed.

"Well, Matthew will come to the house and eat dinners with us, and I'm sure Ma'll insist on serving tea and all that formal stuff. Then later you two can go to socials together, or take walks together, or go sleigh-riding in the winter." She leaned in conspiratorially toward Sophia and confided, "I think that's sooo romantic!" She actually blushed at the confession. "Then if you take to each other, he'll ask Pa for your hand."

Sophia thought about this information for the rest of the morning. After lunch she pulled Abby aside.

"Abby, listen. I think Matthew is a nice young man, but I can't say yes to him courting me."

"Why?" Abby looked genuinely concerned.

"Well. . .because in my religion a girl and a boy aren't allowed to be alone before they're engaged. If Matthew and I were to go to socials and things, we'd be alone in the wagon. . ."

"But you don't have to be alone if you prefer not to. Margaret's sister never went out alone with her beau before they got married, except a couple of times." Abby paused and looked down. "Margaret went with them everywhere."

Sophia didn't know how to comfort Abby. She wished she could think of something wise and useful, but she couldn't, so she went on in a solemn tone, "But also, Muslim girls don't marry people who are not Muslim."

"Oh."

"Yeah."

"But Sophia, there aren't any Muslims here. Are you just supposed to become an old maid?"

"I don't know, Abby. But I haven't given up on my. . .family completely. I may find them someday." She sighed. "So I guess I'll just have to tell your Pa no."

Abby seemed as disappointed as Sophia felt. She smiled weakly at Sophia and they went back in the house.

Telling Mr. Sampson she didn't wish to be courted by Matthew was the hardest thing Sophia'd had to do since she'd arrived. Not just because she liked Matthew, but because Mr. and Mrs. Sampson seemed so caught up in the excitement of her possible courtship that she didn't want to disappoint them. That night, however, she explained that she wasn't ready for courting yet. She asked Mr. Sampson to convey to Matthew that she was honored, but that where she came from girls didn't marry so young, and she didn't feel ready to consider it yet. Since things turned out this way, Sophia was glad she had given him the thank you note. At least he'd understand that she did think highly of him.

ON MONDAY, MR. SAMPSON took Sophia and Abby to the Reeces in the wagon. It wasn't too far, but it wouldn't be fun to walk it. Sophia rode almost the entire way in silence. Her heart was heavy with the knowledge that Mr. Sampson would be turning Matthew away that day. She was frustrated and felt lost in her faith. It wasn't her fault she'd been dumped in the middle of a place where there were no Muslims, and she had no idea when or if she'd ever get back home. It wasn't fair that she couldn't allow herself to fall in love with a man as wonderful as Matthew Collins seemed. But at the same time, she couldn't just throw away her faith. She believed that God rewards those who sacrifice for their faith, and that a believer is blessed when they are thankful in plenty and forebearing through trials. Something inside her kept urging her to be patient, despite her frustration. And so it was that she rode in thoughtful silence to the Reece home that humid July morning.

The Reece place was indeed right near the river, and Sophia was glad for a bit of scenery change. As they got closer to the house, though, she began to wonder. It was a dilapidated, old cabin, with no filling in between the logs, and one desolate window with canvas covering it. The inside was even worse. The Reeces sure were in need of someone to tend the place. Their tin plates were sitting on the table, with the residue of what appeared to be several different meals on them. The dirt floor was dusty and crawling with ants—not swept clean and tidy like the Sampsons'. The bed was just a straw mattress that was in dire need of a beating, and had crumpled blankets all over it, with no pillows. Sophia couldn't tell who slept there, and wondered if they all did because there was no other bed in the place. She hoped there weren't bedbugs in it. Yiiikkhh. The Reeces' dog was a scrawny old thing named Charlie. At the moment, he was wet. He'd probably just come back from swimming in the river. He stank to high heaven.

Mr. Reece hardly greeted Sophia. He was awkward and gruff, and looked like he had walked straight out of the *Beverly Hillbillies*. His clothes were ill-fitting and his pantlegs, which came down only to mid-calf and looked strangely like capris, were uneven and straggly at the bottom. His hair was long and uncombed, and his beard was uneven.

His son was tall and lanky, with red hair and so many freckles that his skin looked blotched. He was cleaner and more put-together looking than his father, and he was kinder as well.

"Mornin' Mr. Sampson. Ladies. Thank you for helpin' us out with Clara."

"Glad to oblige, Stan," said Mr. Sampson. "This is Sophia. Abby will be staying with her the first week or so, until she gets used to being on her own."

"Good to meet you, Miss Sophia. I know the place is in a state. Ma wouldn'a never let it git like this. But Pa don't like to keep house, and I spend most of my time either farmin' or roofin'. Clara here seems to have. . .taken leave of us, so the house han't had no attention a'tall for a good long while."

"That's alright, Stan. It won't take long to whip it back into shape," Sophia said, wondering if she could do that without actually touching anything.

"Do ya need anythin' before we set out?"

"No, I don't think so. Thank you." *A good old pair of latex gloves and some Clorox would be nice,* she thought.

Mr. Sampson chatted with the men for a few minutes and then called Sophia and Abby out to the wagon as he was getting ready to go. He inclined his head toward them and turned his back to the house, speaking quietly. "Girls, if you don't want to do this, it's alright. I'll take you back home with me now. I had no idea Reece had let the house go this far to seed since Elizabeth died."

Abby and Sophia looked at each other. "No, Pa, I think we can handle it. I'll help Sophia get the house into good shape this week and then it won't be hard for her to keep up with," Abby said.

"Well, alright then. I'll come by in the afternoon to check on you."

"Alright."

"Thank you, Mr. Sampson."

As he drove away, Sophia and Abby looked at each other, then at the house, then at each other again. They each took a deep breath and went back inside. Clara was rocking in a chair in the middle of the room. You could see she'd once been a beautiful young woman. She had long, deep red hair that had been braided into two plaits on the sides of her head, and hung limply almost to her lap. Her faded calico dress was a bit big on her—it must have been her mother's. She held a feather in one hand and toyed with it with the other. Her hands looked far older than she did—they were worn and weathered. But her face was porcelain white and draped with beautiful little freckles. There wasn't a wrinkle or other blemish on it, and her back was straight and dignified, just like Adoeet's, even in her current state of injury and melancholy.

The girls found an old cornstalk broom sticking out from the side of the bed. It was so dry it cracked when Abby began to sweep. The girls would have to make a new one. Sophia went down to the river and got some water for the dishes. It wasn't as clean as the well water from home, but it would have to do. She boiled it in the iron pot that sat on top of an iron stand in the fireplace. She hated to have to stoke up the fire—it was already blazing hot in that heavy, July kind of way—but she had no choice. There was no way cold water would get all the muck off of those dishes.

The girls took the mattress outside and beat it with a fireplace poker and the side of an ax. It was even filthier than it had looked inside. They left it to air out and went to see what they could fix to eat. They looked in the larder and found precisely nothing. There was some cornmeal in the barrel, so they made cornbread and ate it with some dried venison from the smokehouse, which was out behind the house. They vowed to bring their lunches from now on. They were afraid to drink the river water, and so just went thirsty. Clara took the plate they gave her, but only managed to eat a few bites. They talked to her, coaxed her, offered her their own cornbread, but she just stared with a haughty, angry gaze. They weren't sure what to do, so they left the plate with her and went back to cleaning the house. Sophia attacked the table with a scrub brush and Abby went to get some corn stalks to make the new broom.

Mr. Sampson came to check on them shortly after lunch. He was impressed by how much work they'd gotten finished, and he tried speaking a few minutes with Clara, although she didn't answer him, of course. He said he'd be back before sundown to pick them up.

All the time Abby and Sophia were working, Clara sat rocking, staring blankly at her feet. She didn't make any sound and she didn't move when Abby swept near her. So Abby just left the spot where her chair was and swept around her.

After lunch, Sophia and Abby made another batch of cornbread for the men to eat when they came home, and then they sat outside in the grass. It was so hot, they dunked their sunbonnets in the river, then wrung them out and put them back on wet.

Thankfully, Mr. Reece and Stan got home right before Mr. Sampson arrived to take the girls home. At least they didn't have to sit around with the men for long. Stan was kind and appreciative of all the girls' work, but Mr. Reece barely grunted his thanks.

When they got home, Mrs. Sampson had rabbit stew and fresh cucumbers and radishes for them. The girls went to bed exhausted.

"The rest of the summer won't be as hard as today was," Abby commented as they lay in bed. "You won't have all that catch-up cleaning to do."

"Yeah," replied Sophia. "Maybe you can teach me to knit tomorrow. I'm going to need something to keep me busy."

14

URING THAT WEEK, SOPHIA and Abby whipped the Reece house into tip-top shape, and Stan Reece spent most of his time roofing the Sampsons' house. Sophia did the cooking at the Reece's, made butter, and carried well water to the wagon—she had to load up two buckets on the yolk before they left home in the mornings and carry them into the Reece house, so they would have fresh well-water to drink and cook with. Abby did the dishes, swept the floor, and kept the place tidy. Thank God, they didn't have to wash the Reeces' clothing. Mr. Reece had a neighbor lady who did that for them in exchange for fresh milk, which the men took with them every other day or so and dropped at her house.

Abby begged to be able to stay with Sophia permanently and help out at the Reeces. Her mom said she could go most days if the girls made sure the chores were done at home, and she'd have to stay some days to help with the new house. On the days Sophia was there alone, she began taking the Reeces' shotgun out and trying to shoot small game with it. It was heavier than the Sampsons', but she managed to get it to her shoulder. She often saw turkeys, rabbits, and squirrels, but wasn't practiced enough to hit them yet. She kept at it, though, hoping to surprise the men with fresh meat one evening.

Clara was pretty far along in her physical recovery. She could make it to the outhouse and back by herself, and as soon as the place was clean, her demeanor and facial expression relaxed a bit. She even spent one afternoon singing an Indian lullaby, so the girls knew she could speak. She probably didn't remember any English, though. Sophia was reminded of Adoeet's preference for sitting alone, and wondered if this was a common Native American trait. Mrs. Sampson had said they weren't with the same tribe, but they sure had similar habits. In any case, Sophia and Abby talked to her as they worked, and sat near her when they were talking about their grand plan to help the Jordans' slaves, which they hadn't entirely given up on. They also had begun speaking of ways to help Adoeet, although those seemed more limited. Sophia knew there was an Underground Railroad for slaves, but wasn't aware of any way they could return Adoeet to his tribe—or even if they'd take him back once he got there.

⚜ ⚜ ⚜

One Thursday, the girls were just cleaning up after lunch when the Reeces' wagon came bumping across the field. It was coming toward them at a full gallop and the girls were terrified that the horses had been spooked—they were running pell-mell toward them. Abby had told Sophia when she taught her to ride that you have to be careful about horses when heading home—they'll break out into a run if you let them, they're so eager to get home to a brush and some oats. But this didn't look like jaunty horses happy to be home. This looked like panic.

As the wagon got closer, they saw that Mr. Reece was alone on the wagon seat. He was frantically waving one arm and calling the girls. Sophia hadn't even realized he knew their names.

The rickety old wagon pulled to an abrupt halt in front of the cabin. The horses had a hard time stopping, they had been galloping so hard. Mr. Reece jumped down and went to the wagonbed.

As the girls approached the wagon, they saw that Stan was lying on his back, flat against the wagon boards. His face was swollen and pale, his freckles standing out in stark contrast to his white skin. He appeared to be unconscious, or worse.

"What happened?" Sophia asked.

"Yellow jackets. Damn things swarmed on 'im when he stepped on their nest out by the edge of the small cornfield. There weren't very many of 'em, but as soon as they started stingin' he got woozy. He sat down on the back of the wagon and then passed out. Said his face was tinglin'." As he spoke, Mr. Reece climbed into the wagon and squatted next to Stan.

Sophia jumped in and looked at him. There were about 10 stings on his face and forearms. They were fiery red in the center and swelling up around the edges. If his face was that swollen, Sophia knew that his throat was also probably swelling inside. There wasn't much time.

"When did this happen?"

"Not five minutes ago. We was just near here, on the other side of the cornfield."

A strange, efficient calm came over Sophia. "Alright, listen. Mr. Reece, go get me cold water from the river. Abby, can you ride bareback?"

"Yes, if I have to."

"OK. Mr. Reece, give her one of the horses. Abby, ride home and get my backpack as fast as you can. It's in the trunk at the foot of the bed."

"Backpack?"

"My satchel."

"Alright."

As they spoke, Mr. Reece had already started

to unhitch one of the horses. He actually helped Abby up onto it, and she set off. Sophia turned her attention back to Stan. His breathing was labored. Sophia opened his mouth. She couldn't see well enough to tell if his airway was swollen or how badly, but as she watched he sputtered once and then didn't breathe any more at all. Sophia tilted his head back and put her hand underneath his neck. She pinched his nose and began to breathe into his mouth. She had to exhale strongly but she was able to get some air down his throat. Mr. Reece brought the cold water and just stood by, wringing his hands. Sophia felt for a pulse. She couldn't find one, but that wasn't unusual – she hadn't been able to find one on her partner in CPR class either, and she had been in perfect health. But Stan's wrist was cold and clammy. She put her head on his chest. She did hear a faint heartbeat, so she just kept up the breathing. Mr. Reece's eyes were wide as he watched Sophia work.

"Oh, dear Lord, not Stan, too. I can't take this, dammit! Please. Please don't take him," Mr. Reece fretted and prayed as he paced back and forth at the foot of the wagon.

Sophia kept breathing for Stan at a slow and steady pace. It was getting a bit more difficult to force the air into his lungs, and Sophia knew his airway was closing up tighter. She looked up but didn't see Abby yet.

"*Bismillah Alaik!* " she prayed in Arabic. God

help you! "Hang on, Stan!"

The next time she listened to his heart, it was even fainter, and it was irregular, now, too, but it was still beating. She kept breathing and looked again for Abby. There she was—a small speck on the horizon.

By the time Abby arrived, Sophia was shaking and lightheaded. As soon as Abby pulled up and slid off the lathered horse, she grabbed the backpack from her. There inside, where she had packed it back into the first aid kit that day—it seemed forever ago—was her Epi-pen. She dug it out and broke off the gray endcap. Squatting beside Stan she said *"Bismillah"* one more time and jabbed the black tip into his thigh, through his trousers. She held the Epi-pen in place for about ten seconds. "Please, *ya Allah!* Let this work!" she begged.

She removed the Epipen and massaged Stan's leg at the injection site for several seconds. Then she checked the black tip of the pen and, sure enough, the needle was visible. That meant the medicine had been delivered. Sophia knew well that the next step should be to call 911. But since her cell phone didn't reach into the 21st century, she hoped the Benadryl in her bag would get Stan through the worst of the shock, if he would just wake up and be able to take it.

Sophia went back to breathing for Stan. It got easier, and soon the warmth returned to his skin.

When she listened to his heart it was stronger and more regular. "*Alhamdulillah!*" she said, and sat back onto the wagonbed. She looked up with a sigh of relief. When she did so, she found Abby and Mr. Reece staring at her with a mixture of awe and bewilderment on their faces.

Uh-oh.

But before she had to come up with some explanation, Stan began to stir. He tried to sit up right away and Sophia settled him back down.

"What happened?" he asked.

You were stung by yellow jackets."

"Oh, yeah. I was lookin' at that corn. . ." His words were thick and slurred.

"It's alright now, Stan. You're going to be OK," Sophia assured him. "But don't try to talk just yet. Your throat's still swollen. Mr. Reece, can you get me a cup full of that well water we brought?" Sophia asked Abby to get the river water Mr. Reece had brought earlier and start sponging Stan's face with it—mostly because Abby looked like she needed something to do. Her face was almost as pale as Stan's. Sophia didn't know that her own face was flushed red with fear and effort.

When Mr. Reece brought the water, Sophia and Abby helped Stan sit up. Then Sophia dug into her backpack and came up with the box of Benadryl. She emptied the powder from two of the pink and white capsules into the cup and had him drink it all. At first, he had trouble swallowing—

both because his throat was swollen and because the powder was bitter—but Sophia urged him to try and get it all down. Eventually he did. Then Sophia asked Mr. Reece to get him into the shade. She was shocked to see him pick his grown son up from the wagonbed like a baby, jump down onto the ground, and carry him into the tiny cabin. Abby brought an old blanket from the back of the wagon, rolled it up for a pillow and set it behind his head on the bed.

Sophia caught sight of Mr. Reece glancing furtively from Stan to the horse Abby had ridden. The poor thing was lathered and panting. Sophia could tell that Mr. Reece didn't know whether to take care of the animal or stay with Stan. "Go ahead and water him, Mr. Reece. Stan is going to be alright, I think." Mr. Reece glanced at her once more, almost suspiciously, and then, back to his old self, grunted and moved off with the horse.

"Sophia, that was amazing. What was that you put in his leg?" Abby demanded in amazement.

"Ummm. . .I'll explain it to you later. Right now we need to make sure there aren't any more stingers left in his skin."

Abby began pouring over Stan's arm and face, taking out one stinger from his forearm and two from his face. Sophia didn't find any in the arm that was on her side of Stan, but she did find one is his cheek, one in his neck and one on his temple. Sophia and Abby got all the stingers out, and by then Stan had fallen back to sleep, his breathing easy and rhythmic. The high excitement and adrenaline faded, leaving Sophia exhausted. She smiled, though, at the way Abby had gone back to sponging Stan's red, swollen face. It looked as if Abby were developing feelings for Stan, although she'd never expressed an interest in him before. Maybe it was just the drama of the moment.

As she thought about it, Mr. Sampson drove up in his own wagon. Mr. Reece met him outside and told him that Stan had been stung by yellow jackets. Mr. Sampson dashed inside and found the girls tending Stan. He rushed over to check on all three. Abby explained what had happened, and told him how Sophia had "saved his life." Sophia demurred and looked meaningfully at Abby, hoping to escape explaining her methods. It worked for the moment.

Mr. Sampson and the girls stayed just awhile longer and made sure Stan was as comfortable as possible. Sophia gave Mr. Reece six more Benadryl and instructed him to give Stan two at sunset, two more in the night, and two at dawn. She hoped she wouldn't run out of them before he was out of the woods. There were 16 left.

On the way home, Abby asked again what Sophia had given Stan.

"I promise I'll tell you all about it when we're alone," Sophia told her. "It's a long story." She wouldn't be able to keep her truth away from Abby any longer, and she was glad.

That night after the candle was out, as Sophia lay in bed, something occurred to her. She bolt upright and said, "*Ya Allah!*"

"What is it?" asked Abby, taken aback.

"Abby! There was something tugging at my mind all afternoon and I couldn't put my finger on it. Now I've got it!! It was Clara!"

"Clara?"

"Yes! Did you see her? When we put Stan in the bed, she turned around in her chair and watched Mr. Reece lay him down." It was the first time Clara had indicated that she saw or understood what was going on around her.

"No! I didn't see her. Oh, my goodness!"

"I knew it. I knew she was in there somewhere."

THE NEXT DAY WAS Friday. The girls
got up early and did all Abby's chores,
so Mrs. Sampson agreed to let her go
with Sophia to the Reeces. Sophia was
glad to have the whole day alone with Abby, so
she could explain her strange situation. She took
her backpack with her to the Reeces so her words
would have the solid backing of her cell phone,
her photo album and her other things. But when
they arrived, their discussion was delayed yet again.
Stan had spiked a fever.

Sophia knew that was common with insect
stings, and would have given everything she
owned (which admittedly wasn't much!) for some
antibiotics. Stan was shivering on his straw bed in
the hot, stuffy cabin, his teeth chattering. When
Sophia felt him, she pulled her hand away quickly.
He was burning up.

Mr. Reece had Stan covered with the blanket

from the wagon and a couple of horse blankets as well, but Sophia knew this wasn't the right thing to do. She had heard her grandmother tell of being put in a tub of ice cold Damascus spring water to bring down her fever when she was a child. But Sophia didn't have any water that cold. She asked Mr. Reece to bring in the buckets of well water from the wagon.

As he was carrying them in, Sophia took the blankets off of Stan. He shivered and begged to be covered again.

"I'm sorry, Stan. We have to get your fever down. I know this will be difficult, but you've got to trust me." Stan shivered and curled himself up into a ball.

"Abby, take off your apron. We'll dunk it in the water and sponge it onto Stan."

"Are you sure, Sophia?" Abby was incredulous. "You're supposed to keep people warm when they have a fever. It sweats the fever out of them."

"No, the sweat comes after the fever breaks, Abby. Mr. Reece, I'm asking you to trust me. I don't know how bad Stan's fever is, and I don't have all the medicines I need to help him, so I don't know how much good it will do, but I promise you, I do know what I'm doing. Cooling him is the right thing to do." *After all, her grandmother was still around, so it must have worked for her!*

"Alright," Mr. Reece said, and Abby nodded. Sophia had credibility in the medical department.

"If only I had some ice!" Sophia fretted.

Mr. Reece piped up. "I can get you some ice. Johnson's in Westport has an ice house."

Sophia calculated the time. It would take him a good hour and a half, both ways, even on horseback. But it was the only chance they had, and besides, it would keep Mr. Reece busy doing something helpful.

"Alright, good. Mr. Reece, you go get the ice. Bring as much as you can carry—Oh, my God, how will you carry it?!"

"I got me a big saddlebag. I'll bring as big a chunk as I can fit in it."

"OK, good. Abby and I'll keep wetting him down until you get back. Did you give him his medicine this morning?" "Yah, at sunrise, just like you said."

Sophia looked out the paneless window. It had to be about 9:00 by now. She got the cup and gave Stan another two Benadryl. She made him drink the whole thing, and he must have been delirious because he muttered, "Clara! I'm gonna tell Ma." The girls worked hard to sponge him off; he kept fighting them, trying to curl up and stay warm.

After about a half hour, the Benadryl took effect. Stan calmed down and fell into a fitful sleep.

"Sophia, you promised you'd tell me about the medicine from yesterday," Abby reminded her as she continued to sponge Stan's face and arms.

So the moment of truth had come.

"OK. Abby," Sophia began, retrieving her backpack from the doorway where she'd leaned it when they'd arrived. "What I'm going to tell you will sound very strange. Believe me, it's still a little strange for me. But I swear to you that it is true. So please don't think I'm crazy."

Abby didn't say anything, just waited for Sophia to go on. "OK," she repeated. "First of all, I'm not really from New York," Sophia tested the waters.

"Alright. . ." Abby obviously wasn't quite sure what to think.

"So where are you from?"

Sophia almost laughed. It sounded so absurd to say it out loud. "I'm from the future."

"What?" Abby sounded almost irritated.

"I swear it. I'm from Kansas City, but not now. When I fell in the river it was May 29, 2013. When I came out of the river I was here with you, in 1857."

"Well, what did you come for? How did you get here?" Abby's voice carried challenges as well as questions.

"I didn't come for anything. I didn't do it on purpose. One day I was on an outing with my family along the river, and it was really high and rushing fast. I fell in and was swept downstream. All that part of what I told you is true. But when I came up, I found myself here, in 1857. I have no idea how it happened."

Abby dunked the apron back in the water and wrung it out as she spoke. "Are you sure, Sophia?

Maybe you just hit your head and forgot your real past, then made one up."

"No, Abby. In fact, I wish that were true. But look," she reached for her backpack, "I have proof." Sophia opened the zipper and Abby stared at it.

"What?" asked Sophia when she saw the look on Abby's face.

"What's that? I never noticed that on your bag."

"What's what? Oh, the zipper? That's just a way to close the bag. Joshua liked it, too." She reached in and brought out her cell phone. Its battery had long since died, which was a shame, because the ring tones and digital screen would really have convinced Abby. She handed it to her, though, dead as it was.

"What is it?"

"It's a cell phone. Back home, almost everyone has one."

"What do you do with it?"

Sophia had never thought about the fact that the purpose of a phone wouldn't be immediately obvious to someone in 1857.

"Well, you call each other with it."

"Call each other?"

Wow. Sophia realized she'd have to start at the very beginning.

"You push those numbered buttons, and then the other person—they have a phone, too—their phone rings, like that triangle they used for the chopping contest at the fourth of July, remember? Then they say, "Hello?" and you can hear them, no matter how far away you are. Like a telegraph except without wires, and with voice instead of just clicks." She put the phone to Abby's ear. "See? You listen from the ear part and when you talk they can hear you."

"Hello?" Abby said into the phone. "I don't hear anyone."

"Well, it's dead. The batteries are dead." Abby looked at her quizzically.

"It doesn't work anymore. There isn't anyone to talk to here. No one else has one."

Abby seemed to understand that concept.

"And look at this." Sophia dug down into the bottom of the outside pocket and came up with six pennies, a quarter, and two dimes. The quarter was one of the state coins, Vermont, and Sophia showed Abby the picture of the man gathering sap from Maple trees. The date underneath read, "2001." The dates on the other coins ranged from 1964 to 2007.

Abby looked at Sophia as she held the coins in her hand. "My stars, Sophia. Are you really from the future?"

"Totally, dude," replied Sophia, in her best surfer accent. Abby cocked her head. "Yes," Sophia laughed. "I am."

Abby jumped to another next question.

"So what about the medicine we're giving Stan?

And what was that thing you stabbed him with?"

Sophia pulled out her medicines. "When I fell in the river, I was on a bike ride with my family. Bikes are sort of like small wagons that you pedal yourself. . .I guess you don't have them yet. . .but all the things I had put in my backpack came with me." She showed Abby the different boxes, pill bottles, and ointments. "This is Imodium. It's for diarrhea. I took it for a couple of days after I first arrived because the well water made me sick. This is Tylenol. It's for—" Sophia looked up at Abby. "Oh, MY GOD!! Abby, bring me the cup. Fill it with water again."

Abby started to comply. "Why?"

"Oh, my God. I can't believe I forgot this. This is Tylenol. It is like aspirin. Do you know aspirin?"

"Aspirin? I don't think so."

"Well, this will take away Stan's fever. It won't fix the infection or whatever is causing the fever, but it will lower his temperature and make him feel better." Sophia thought. "The problem is that these pills are solid. He'll have to swallow them whole. Or else we'll have to grind them up. See if you can find anything in the kitchen we can grind with."

Abby looked but, as they had suspected, there was nothing. "Well, I'm sure he won't be able to swallow them. His throat is too swollen and he's never swallowed a pill before, I bet. Hmmm." Sophia went outside and found a small rock, about the size of a golf ball. One end of it was pointy. Then she took the cup outside and poured water over it. Not sterile, but as clean as she could manage. Back inside she put two Tylenol inside the cup and began smashing them with the rock. It was slow going because the rock didn't ever seem to hit the pills straight on. They bounced around in the bottom of the cup several times, but eventually Sophia got them ground down to a manageable size. She put a couple of tablespoonfuls of water into the cup and stirred with her finger. Then she walked over to Stan.

"Here, Stan. Drink this." She shook him a bit and Abby lifted his head off the bed. They got as much of the bitter liquid down him as they could. It was really a challenge this time, because he was so fitful, being half asleep, and the Tylenol was apparently even nastier than the Benadryl had been. But he got enough down to satisfy Sophia. She refilled the cup with pure water and had him drink some of that.

Sophia whispered the prayer she'd always said when taking medicine, "*Bismillah ir Rahman ir Raheem, La hawla wa la quwwata illah bi lah,*" "In the name of God, Most Gracious, Most Merciful, There is no power nor authority except with God." Then she added "*Laysa laha min dooni lahi kashifa.*" No one less than God can remove this. She couldn't believe she'd let Stan lie there all morning with a fever, when she had Tylenol right there in her backpack.

When Stan had settled back down, Abby drew Sophia's attention back to the used syringe. "This is my Epi-pen. When I was about six years old, I was stung by a bee. My throat swelled up and my parents had to take me to the hospital. I passed out, like Stan. So ever since then, I've had to carry that thing with me when I'm outdoors, just in case. It's medicine that is delivered through a needle. The medicine stops your body from reacting to the sting."

"Joshua was stung by a bee once, and he didn't pass out like Stan. He didn't need that medicine."

"Well, not everyone is allergic to stings. Most people do just fine when they are stung by a bee or something. But a few people react like Stan did. It can actually kill them. If we hadn't had it, Stan might have died, because his throat was swelling shut."

"Thank God you had it!" The girls sat in silence for a few seconds, Abby looking down at Stan, and Sophia again had the feeling that she was sweet on him. Then Abby lightened the mood. "So anyway," she ventured, "Tell me more about the future."

Where could she even begin?

"Well, first let me show you a bit of it." Sophia got out her photo album.

The girls settled down with Abby wiping Stan's brow and face again.

"These are pictures of me and my family and

friends." She opened the album.

"Tintypes!" exclaimed Abby. "Gosh, they look so real!"

"In my time we have pictures that move, too. You can record someone running a race, for example, and then watch the whole thing again later. I could do it on my phone if it was working."

"Mr. and Mrs. Duncan had a tintype portrait made of themselves before they came out West. I wish I had one of Olivia."

"Me, too," said Sophia sympathetically. "I would love to see her." She handed the album to Abby, opened to the first picture.

"This is my friend, Amani. This was taken at our school. See the desks?" It didn't look too much different than any school Abby might have already seen. She nodded, not too impressed.

"That's my brother." Sophia ran her finger over Hisham's face, laughing out at her from the photo. She hadn't looked at these pictures since shortly after she'd arrived. "And this is my bird, Kuzko. This was taken in my mom's room." Sophia's eyes moved from the green parrot to the background. "Look! There's the ceiling fan. See the lights? They're electric."

"Electric?"

"Umm. . .automatic. You just touch a button on the wall and they come on. You don't have to light them or anything."

"Gosh." Abby squinted at the picture. Sophia

turned the page.

"This is my family outside our house. That's my Grandpa, Grandma, mom, and dad. These are my friends, Jenan, Sarah, and Amani."

"How come everyone is wearing a scarf except your grandma?"

"Well. . .she isn't Muslim."

"I thought everyone must be Muslim in your time?"

"No," Sophia laughed. "Actually, most people in America are Christian, like you."

"Oh." Abby seemed puzzled at that.

They went through the entire album, and as they did Abby's sense of awe grew, until they reached the last picture, when Sophia's case for proving her future existence was cinched.

"Oh, look. This is Amani and me washing my dad's car." The picture showed the two girls, scarves and sweatsuits wet with soapy water, waving at the camera. Amani had the hose in her hand and Sophia was standing by the open Land Rover door. The angle was so good that you could even see inside the car a bit—the steering wheel was visible, and a small bit of the dashboard.

"What is THAT?" asked Abby.

"That is a car. When they were first invented they were called 'horseless carriages.' See? You sit there and you steer with that," she explained, pointing inside the car.

"What makes it go, then, if not horses?"

"Gasoline. It's like the electric lights. It's automatic. It's all machinery. I don't know exactly how it works."

"So that's why you didn't know how to ride a horse!"

Sophia giggled. "Almost no one has horses in my time. Everyone uses cars. It's even illegal to ride a horse in the streets, I think."

"Gosh" was all Abby could think of to say. She pointed to Amani's white scarf, standing out in stark contrast to her dark face. "She's a Negro?"

"Yes."

"And she's your best friend? Is she. . ..a slave?"

Sophia looked at her and blinked. "No. We don't have slavery anymore. It was stopped right after. . .uhhh. . .in about 1865."

"Really? So Kansas does enter the union as a free state?"

Sophia had to be careful here. She didn't want to tell Abby about the Civil War. "Yes, it does. But in 1865, all the slaves are freed by President Lincoln, even the ones in the South."

"Abraham Lincoln? The one who debated Stephen Douglas last year?"

"Yes! The same one. He becomes president."

"Gosh," Abby said again. She reached out and touched Sophia's face, to make sure she was real. "Oh my God, Sophia, how did this happen?"

"I have no idea." They looked at each other. Sophia hoped she hadn't gone too far, telling Abby so many details about the future. But Abby was focused on more immediate issues.

"Was that the only bee medicine you had?"

"Yes."

"So what if *you* get stung by something?"

Sophia actually hadn't thought of that yet. It was something that would have cost her sleep before, worrying about what would happen if she got stung now that her Epi-pen was an empty pen. "Well, I guess we just have to pray that I don't." And when she said it, she honestly wasn't scared.

As they sat there, Abby trying to digest the news she had just learned and Sophia pondering the incredible odds of her having *just* the thing Stan needed, reinforcing her instinctual belief that Allah had a plan for her being here, Stan began to stir. The girls looked down to find him sweating profusely.

"It's hot," he said. Sophia and Abby smiled at each other.

Sophia felt his head, wishing she was as expert at measuring fevers as her mother. Her mother could tell what someone's temperature was just by touching her cheek to their forehead.

It was definitely cooler, and the girls helped him sit up.

"May I have some water?" he asked. He really was more polite than his dad.

Abby got the tin cup and refilled it. As she handed it to him, Sophia saw her smile in a bashful sort of way.

As Abby watched, Sophia put all her things back into her backpack and sat it on the floor, out of Stan's line of sight. "Abby," she said quietly, "Let's not tell anyone else about this yet. I don't know if it's a good idea for people to know."

"You might be right. I won't say anything."

By the time Mr. Reece galloped up, Stan was perfectly awake and just finishing his water. When his dad saw him, he half scowled. "Whaddama gonna do with all this ice?" he asked, and stomped out to feed and water his horse. Sophia was sure his gruff manner was hiding a lot of relief. She hoped Stan was really on the mend, and that it wasn't just the Tylenol masking the symptoms. He fell back to sleep, restfully this time.

While Abby kept an eye on Stan, Sophia turned to Clara. As she talked to Abby about Kansas City circa 2013, she took out Clara's braids and brushed her hair. When she was finished rebraiding it she squatted right in front of the rocker.

"I know you're in there, Clara. Please talk to me." To her surprise, Clara looked straight at her and said a whole sentence—in her Indian tongue. Sophia had no idea what she had said, but she hugged her anyway and then the girls went out on the front step to wait for Mr. Sampson. They were eager to report the good news on both their charges. In the fading sunlight, they watched Mr. Sampson drive up, and soon realized that Matthew was with him on the wagon seat. Suddenly Sophia was nervous.

"Matthew came by to return my clothes this afternoon and I told him about Stan," Mr. Sampson explained.

"I asked if I could come along and see him. I hope you ladies don't mind the intrusion," he said, looking down at his hat, which was in his hands.

"Not at all," said Abby, for Sophia hadn't yet found her voice.

"Stan's doing much better. I'm sure he'll be glad to see you.

Matthew inclined his head toward the girls and ducked through the cabin door, which was a bit shorter than his own frame. He visited with Stan while the girls loaded the well buckets into the back of the wagon. Then they went inside to say goodbye.

"Here are my nurses now." Stan said as the girls walked in. They both blushed.

"I'm glad you're feeling better, Stan." Sophia told him. Then she retrieved her backpack from the corner and took some more Tylenol and Benadryl from the outer pocket. As she did so, she caught sight of Stan. His smile as he chatted with Matthew was forced and he seemed uncomfortable. That was odd. "Here are your medicines for the rest of the night," she told him. "This kind is only for fever, so don't take it unless the fever comes back." She looked at Mr. Reece. "You'll have to grind it in the cup, unless he can chew it or swallow it whole. Here's the cup and rock I used."

"Thank you kindly, Miss Sophia," Stan answered for his Pa.

On the way back home, Matthew put Sophia more at ease. He was very easy to talk to and seemed genuinely concerned for Stan.

"Mr. Reece says you saved Stan's life with that medicine of yours, Miss Sophia. I'm sure glad you were there." Sophia looked at Abby. "Yes, it really was a blessing."

"My pa had a similar experience when he was younger. Seems he was out trappin' back East one winter, and he spilled boiling water on his hand while he was skinning an antelope. After a few days it got worse instead of better, and Pa started to get feverish. Then this Injun just happened upon his camp. Pa normally wouldn'tve been there that time of day, but there he was, lying in his tent, with the antelope skinned but not dressed, hanging from its tree branch, not knowin' whether to freeze or rot. Pa was terrified – said farewell to his scalp - but that Injun just came up to him real silent and looked at his hand. Then he picked him and carried him over his shoulder back to his camp. The medicine man there put some juice from a plant on his burn, then wrapped it up and gave Pa a pipe to smoke. The pipe smoke made him sleepy, and next thing he knew he was waking up in the tent of a family with two small children. The squaw had been taking care of him, I guess. His clothes were clean—he always wondered how they got them off him and back on—and his hand was almost healed. He waited til nighttime and then hightailed it back to his tent. His antelope was gone. He figured the Injuns had taken it. He still has the scar where that water burned him."

"That's amazing!" said Abby.

Sophia wondered if the plant they had used was Aloe Vera. She knew that people back home said it was an old Indian remedy for burns.

"What tribe were the Indians?" asked Sophia.

"Oh, I don't know. Shawnee, maybe. They're all the same, aren't they?"

Sophia was taken aback by this comment, but she put it and his use of the term "Injun" down to nineteenth-century sensibilities. There was an awful lot of propaganda against the Indians in the newspapers, and on the tongues of settlers.

When they got home, Mrs. Sampson invited Matthew for dinner, and the evening was passed very pleasantly. Matthew was his easy, affable self. Sophia decided to stop taking everything so seriously and began to relax, too.

On Saturday, Sophia told Abby more about the future she remembered. She told her about TV and the Internet, and airplanes, and about her grandparents in Syria. Abby asked very intelligent questions.

"Is the United States still the United States?"

"How come you are Muslim and most of the people aren't?"

"What do you eat, if you don't live on farms?"

Stan stayed home for just one more day, and then returned to the field. Mr. Reece was just as quiet as ever with Sophia and Abby, but a lot less gruff. He never thanked them directly, but the girls knew he was grateful to them for saving Stan.

After the day Stan was stung, Sophia and Abby tried several times to rouse Clara again. They talked to her about her brother, asked her questions about her childhood, and even mentioned family incidents that Stan had told them about. She responded sometimes, always in her Indian tongue, and even started a couple of "conversations" with the girls, but never spoke in English. Her leg was still weak from sitting still for so long after her injury, but she began taking small walks, making her way to the river occasionally. The first time she did this, Sophia was shocked and watched her closely the whole way, ready to spring if Clara should fall. But she walked gracefully along the river, carrying the tattered feather with her. Sophia wondered what its significance was. She began to wonder if Clara was another reason she had been brought to 1857, and somehow in the back of her mind believed that if Clara would just come back to herself completely, then she would be transported home, although wanting to go home was more habit now than anything else.

Except for seeing her parents and family again, Sophia wasn't entirely sure she even wanted to return. She missed some things, like the Internet, hamburgers, and washing machines, but overall she was happy where she was. She was happy not to be bombarded with fast and furious information 24/7. She hadn't realized how overstimulating modern life was until she was able to see it from her place in a simpler, slower time. She liked the quiet lifestyle of the pioneers. The work of living was hard, but at least it was immediate and meaningful, and long summer evenings snapping peas were more relaxing than watching movies or going shopping.

Of course, there was always Matthew, too. Try as she might, Sophia could not avoid thinking about him. She wondered what she was to do if she really was stuck permanently in a long-ago time with no Muslims around. Should she consider telling Matthew her secret and talking to him about Islam?

🌾🌾🌾

About a week after Stan was stung, Sophia bagged her first game. She was sitting in front of the cabin watching Clara walk by the river when she saw a rabbit hopping nearby. She retrieved the Reeces' shotgun, but by the time she made it back outside, it was gone. So when Clara returned to her rocker, Sophia took the gun down to the river and just sat on the bank. Sure enough, she soon spotted another rabbit. She took careful aim, which was a bit awkward in a sitting position, and took her shot. She was as shocked as the rabbit to see it tumble backward a few paces. It hopped just a few times and then lay on the ground. When Sophia got to it, it was almost dead. She said *Bismillah*, picked it up by the ears, and took it to the house. Now that she'd killed it, she wasn't sure what to do with it. It was still a few hours until Mr. Reece and Stan would be home, and she didn't know how to skin or dress it. The excitement went out of her surprise. She was sure the rabbit would go bad if she let it set all afternoon.

She was about to take it out to the smokehouse to protect it from flies when Clara stood up, held out her hand, and took the rabbit out to an old stump. To Sophia's alarm, she produced a knife from the waist sash of her gingham dress and replaced it with her favorite feather. Then she started to matter-of-factly skin the rabbit. She never spoke the whole time she worked and when the rabbit was dressed she gave it to Sophia to cook. Then she washed in the river and sat back down in the rocker, as straight and silent as ever.

After that, whenever Sophia managed to shoot something, Clara would dress it. Stan and Mr. Reece were taken aback a bit in the beginning, but the first taste of the rabbit stew shut them up, and after that they were glad to have whatever Sophia managed to kill.

NEAR THE END OF the week, Stan told the girls that he and his pa would be harvesting the far wheat field for about ten days.

"You think you'll be alright here, with us so far away?"

Hmmm. . .Sophia *was* a bit uneasy about the men being so far away, especially on the days she and Clara would be alone, but she also had a sudden idea. With all the excitement of Stan's run-in with the yellow jackets and Clara's recovery, the girls hadn't had a chance to talk much about their grand escape plan for Mr. William. She wasn't sure where the Jordans' house was or what Stan's views were on slavery, but ventured to propose her idea. "Mrs. Jordan said that Mr. William could help us out anytime we needed him," she explained.

Stan pursed his lips. "The Jordan place is only about a mile from here. But I don't have anything to pay William with and I don't want to accept his labor for free like that." Ha! He was on the right side of the slavery question.

She told Stan that she wasn't one to use slave labor, either, and explained about her and Abby's plan. Stan was more enthusiastic.

"He could do it easily if they'd let him use a horse. I'll talk to Jordan about it."

Sophia wasn't sure she could really talk Mr. William into trying to escape, but she had to at least try.

"Idiots," Abby said of the Jordans. "They won't suspect a thing."

The next day, Mr. William arrived soon after lunch. "*AsSalaamu Alaikum,*" he said, doffing his hat.

"*Wa Alaikum AsSalaam!*" Sophia responded. "Let me get you some water."

"Oh, you don't have to do that, Miss Sophia!" Mr. William protested. Abby didn't let her, anyway. She jumped up and filled the cup herself. She handed it to him and they sat down at the table.

Sophia decided to ease into the escape subject. "Thank you for checking on us, Mr. William. We didn't ask you here to work, though. We asked you to come so that hopefully you and I can try and understand how we each ended up here."

"Yes, I's been burnin' up with curiosity about how a white Muslim girl came to be out on the prairie in the middle of the New World! I didn't even know there were white Muslims, except the Arabs."

"Well, tell me your story first."

"Oh, you girls don't want to hear all that."

"Yes, we do!"

"My story is a tale." He looked down at his hands. "A tale of a seffish young buck whose seffishness cost him his freedom and his family. It ain't easy to tell, and I 'spect it aint easy to he-ah."

"Please, Mr. William. I've been so shocked by the things I've seen since I arrived here. I need to hear your story."

Mr. William cast the girls a sidelong glance, and then gave in and began. "Well, back home, I warn't a poor slave. I was the son of a rich man. Yessuh, I was schooled at the masjid. I could read and write and recite Qur'an. When I was very small, I sat with the sheikh and listened to him teach the oldah boys. But as I got oldah, I strayed away from religion and learnin'.

"I was a strong young man, not owned by no one or controlled by no one—even by m'self. I'as rich in the material things of our time, but oh Lord, I was poor in spirit. I had three wives and five chi'dren—and I was only 19 ye'ahs old! My first wife was a cousin o'mine. She'as older'n I was, and just as stubborn! She tried hard to control me, but I wouldn't let her. My second wife was the sister of a friend o' mine from the next village over, and she and I got on powerful well. My third wife was the widow of a neighborin' fisherman. We had jus' gotten married when I got m'self taken.

"All my wives had they own huts. My father was a well-to-do man, an elder and a good farmer, yessuh. I knows now that the hard work that made him what he was—and the things he learned from it—was the only things he couldn't share wit' me or give tuh me, but they was the things I needed most. He gave me land with peanut and yam crops, but I missed out on the struggle that teaches a body to love the land. I was lazy and took all my blessings like I had 'em comin' tuh me. That laziness and pride cost me muh life.

"My neighbor come to Miriama's hut one evening—she was my second wife—and made me an offer. He offered to have his fam'ly hep me wit' the harvest o' mah peanuts, if'n I would have my fam'ly hep him. He warn't an elder, but he'as older 'n more settled 'n I was. I was shocked that he'd make an offer like that, 'cause seemed to me that harvestin' peanuts was beneath him and me both. Why, that'as women's work! Servant women! Why should we have oahr own fam'lies, and 'specially oahr own se'ves, bend over in dah sun like that to harvest peanuts? We could both afford to hiah others to do it. Nope, I would not stoop so low as to hahvest mah own peanuts. An' I told him what I thought, too. Oh, I was polite about it, but I did let him know I thought he'as crazy. He tried to show me how wrong I was to think like that. I can remember him to dis day, sittin' on the beautiful earth floor of Miriama's hut. . .African earth. . .eatin' the fish stew and yams that Miriama had made, and tryin' to talk me into acceptin' his offer. He said there was a saying in Islam that there was no good in a city that didn't grow its own grain or weave its own cloth. He said the same was true o' men, that there was no good in a man who didn't sow his own soil. He told me that honest work was good for the soul. I jus' laughed to m'self and thought how old-fashioned 'e was.

"The next week, while he'as harvestin' his peanuts, I set out to visit Miriama's brother in the next village. Muh wives were safe at home, mah chi'dren were wit' them and the oldest was over at the *madrassa*. Hiah'd boys and women from the tribe were busy hahvesting muh crop. I'as bored and restless, o' course, wit' no work to do, and so I set out. On muh way, I was overrun by a band o' white men. Now, we knew about slave traders, but dey'as not as much of a thorn in our sides as they had been in the past. The Brits had outlawed slave runnin', and things had settled down quite a bit. Ther'as still others who captured slaves, like the French, but they usually did it by buyin' or stealin' slaves from warrin' nations. The men who took me was illegal British slave runners.

"O' course normally, even an entire band of white men'd be no match for a Mandinka—even a spoiled farmer!—but these men all had guns, and they shot me with some sort o' med'cine. When I woke up I'as in a stone buildin', and I'll be darned if I warn't shackled to round about ten other people—from other tribes—all hooked together by chains around oahr waists. I washed up in the New World after two months at sea, lookin' fur all the world like a mongrel dog; covered with sores from layin' on the wooden shelves all that time, hahdly alive.

"I'as kept on a small farm neah the coast until I'as stronger and had gained most o' mah weight back. Then I'as sold, ta Massa Jordan's pappy. I's been with the Jordans ever since. Ol' Massa Jordan's long since passed, now.

"So I's spent muh life doin' what I saw as beneath me. I's spent muh life as a slave, hahvesting other people's crops, on accoun' a' muh pride. *Astaghfirullah.*

"I tried to keep up mah faith over he'ah. I begged Allah ta understand that I'd done learned muh lesson. I prayed ever' night that He'd let me wake up back home in the mornin', an' I swore that if 'n He would, I'd be sure to hahvest muh own crops forever. I'd even hahvest other people's crops. But I done always woke up on the Jordan plantation.

"The white men don't care a lick for Islam, and they made us go ta church. They whipped us if 'n they found us praying. I learned to pray inside muh head.

"I married a young girl when I'd been he'ah

about ten ye'ahs. She'as bought by the Jordans when she'as long about 14 ye'ahs ol'. She'as wit' child—her ol' massa's baby. She was so lonely and afeared, I got a soft spot in my heart for 'er. We married and raised that baby as oahr own. She'as a faithful wife, *Allahi ahfezha*. Her name was Filijee, but the Jordans called 'er by the name o' Sally. A couple-a years later when she'as 'round about 8 months pregnant with oahr own child, ol' Massa Jordan's wife took ill. She needed some sort-a treatment, and ta pay for it, the Jordan's sold Filijee and little David. Got extra for 'er on account o' her bein' wit' child, too. I don't know where she went or what happened to 'er. I thought I'd die. Finally, I'd found someone ta love and share the pain o' this life wit, and Allah'd taken her away, too. For a while I quit prayin'. But I neva' really left the faith. I'as jus' hurtin'. After a long spell I went back to the prayer, but I never married again.

"I just ask Allah to forgive me and reward me in *Jennah* for all that I's suffered in this here life because of muh stubborn pride."

Sophia was crying by the time Mr. William finished his story. "I done told you it warn't a pretty story," he said, smiling sadly. "But don't cry, young miss."

"Oh, Mr. William!" Abby was wiping her eyes on her apron.

"Actually, if you promise not ta use it, I'll tell you muh real name. I's Ibrahim. Ibrahim ibn Malik al

Khair."

"*Ibnul Malik?*" Ibn Malik means 'son of the king.' "Were you really a prince?"

"Nawh, jus' a boy whose pappy's name was Malik."

"Well, I am proud and honored to know you, brother. Now let me tell you how I came to be here."

"That'll have to wait for tomorrow, Miss Sophia. I gots ta be gettin' back 'afore they get to wonderin' where I is and why I's been gone so long. I's afraid they won't let me keep comin'. Harvest is comin' up on us and I got lots o' odds & ends ta finish at the Jordan place befo' that happens."

"Alright," Sophia said. "I'll tell you Monday. In the meantime, here, take this cup of water outside and bring it back in."

Mr. William looked puzzled, but long years of unquestioning obedience had conditioned him to obey even strange commands. He took the cup outside without comment.

When he came back in with it, Sophia smiled. "Now you can tell them we made you haul water for us."

Ibrahim ibn Malik al Khair's eyes crinkled up and his whole face laughed. "Miss Sophia, I do believe you are somethin' else!"

Sophia smiled back and gave him salaams.

When he'd gone Abby looked earnestly at

Sophia. "We've got to convince him to escape. I can't stand to see him being owned by people who would sell away his wife and child!"

"Maybe when he hears my story, he'll find the courage to try it." Sophia ventured.

The girls were quiet, each lost in her own thoughts, when Abby broke the silence, speaking something that must have been on her mind for awhile.

"Sophia, can I ask you a question?"

"Sure."

"Why don't you eat pork?"

"Well, the short answer is that God told us not to. He didn't say why. But we can think about possible reasons. One of the boys in my class did a science report on pork last year. He learned that pork carries germs that other meats don't, and it's linked to breast cancer. God knows best what's good for us, so if He says something is not permitted He always has a good reason."

"Is there anything else you don't eat?"

"Well, we don't drink alcohol. Or eat carrion— you know, animals that are already dead."

"Not drinking alcohol is a good idea. Margaret's father drinks. He would sometimes come home drunk and yell at her and her mom. Then he'd stay in bed for a few days and not get any work done. He drinks even more since Margaret died."

"Things like that are a problem in my time, too.

Alcohol causes a lot of car accidents."

"Car accidents?"

"You know, the horseless carriages I told you about."

"Oh, yes. Can I ask you something else?"

"Sure."

"Why do you pray five times a day? And why do you pray on the ground?"

"Well, praying five times a day keeps you connected with God and helps you avoid sins. As for why we pray on the ground, we do it to show our humility before God. That's the way all the Prophets prayed, including Prophet Jesus and Prophet Muhammad, peace be upon them. It involves your entire body in worship, not just your heart or your mind."

"Hmmm. . ." Abby turned pensive but didn't ask any more questions.

That night Sophia took her journal and the ink jar outside and wrote Br. Ibrahim's story under the stars. The moon was almost full and she didn't even need a candle. She wrote out her frustration and sadness that Br. Ibrahim's life, and the lives of so many other slaves, seemed so unfair. She wrote until she was so tired her eyes were crossing and her writing was wriggling all over the page. Then she stood and stretched and went back in to bed.

THE NEXT DAY WAS Saturday. When their morning chores were done and lunch out of the way, the girls helped Mrs. Sampson move a few things from the soddy into the new house. After a dinner of boiled potatoes and carrots served with rabbit meat, the girls filled the evening with knitting lessons. First Abby taught Sophia to cast on, which Sophia remembered learning when she was younger, so that went pretty smoothly. The actual knit stitch was more of a hurdle. Sophia couldn't get the tension right and either did the stitch too close to the points of the needles, so it fell off, or too far away from the points so she had to drag it an inch or more to slide it lopsidedly from the left to the right needle. When she had knit two sloppy rows that looked nothing like her mother's neat stitches, she took a break to pray. As she made her ablutions in the well bucket, she saw Abby peeking at her while her hands flew as she worked on the pair of socks she was making. She stood within Abby's hearing to recite her prayers, so Abby could listen to the recitations in Arabic if she wanted to.

On Monday, Sophia began looking for Mr. William right after lunch. She waited and waited, but he didn't come. Sophia was terrified that she had kept him too long on Friday, and that the Jordans wouldn't let him come anymore. She waited all afternoon, and prayed that he wasn't being beaten or punished. This was one time Sophia sorely missed the conveniences of modern life—like phones. She was dying to pick up the phone, apologize for keeping William so long, and find out what was going on.

Sophia did all the housecleaning, then fidgeted a bit, and finally spilled out her tension to Clara. "What if I got him in trouble, Clara?" she asked of her silent friend, who had undone the beadwork on her leather hair ties and was re-beading it. "I knew I shouldn't have made him tell me his whole life story on his first visit. . .I thought I liked this place, you know? I was happy when it was just me and the Sampson's and you guys. I like doing chores—can you believe that?—and riding horses and seeing so many stars at night. . .I mean, I miss my family but somehow I'm sure that time can't be passing for them. . .and living here is good, too. There's no road rage, no pollution, no billboards. . .and I've learned a lot about myself.

But this place has its own evil. And it's worse than any road rage. Can you imagine enslaving another person? I mean. . .I knew that slavery existed, of course, but somehow the. . ..horridness of it just didn't sink in. And the Native Americans aren't enslaved but they're still mistreated. I feel so guilty! All the blessings of my time were built on the backs of people like Mr. William and Adoeet. . .to people in my time the word "Kiowa" is just the name of a street!"

Clara startled Sophia, who was pacing back and forth, by speaking from her place on the floor. "Kiowa?" she asked, plain as day.

Sophia stared at her. "Yes, Kiowa. You know, Adoeet's tribe."

"Adoeet?"

"Yes, he's that young Indian boy the Duncans adopted. You probably haven't seen him. He's blind and scarred from the small pox. He's so regal and dignified, and the children make fun of him."

"Adoeet? Kiowa?"

Sophia nodded. "Yes."

Clara spat on the dirt floor of the cabin and went back to her beading.

Sophia stared at her. This was too much.

"Clara?" Sophia squatted down and shook her shoulders. "Clara! Why did you do that? Why did you spit like that? Does your tribe hate the Kiowas?"

Clara spat again.

"Oh, great," moaned Sophia. "Not only do whites hate blacks and Indians, but the Indians hate each other, too."

That night, as soon as she got home, Sophia asked Abby about it. Abby didn't know why she might have reacted that way.

Sophia was stumped and frustrated. She attacked the cornbread batter with gusto while Abby peeled potatoes. Sophia's mind was in turmoil, trying to sort out the different prejudices around her, so she was distracted when Abby interrupted her thoughts.

"I was ponderin' on what you told me about Olivia," Abby began.

Sophia looked up at her as she slid the cornbread into the oven. Abby's back was turned and she was still peeling away. Sophia didn't know what to expect.

"I'd like to know more about your faith." Abby stopped peeling and looked sheepishly at Sophia, as if she'd asked something rude.

Sophia's mind began to swirl all over again. It was hard to switch gears this fast. Where should she begin? Then she remembered a piece of advice given by the Prophet Mohammad himself, "Begin with the Oneness of God. If they believe that, then tell them about the prayer. If they do that, then ask them to pay charity." So she recited for Abby one of the short chapters of the Qur'an. The chapter that sums up what Muslims believe about the nature of God:

Say: He is Allah, the One and Only Allah,
the Eternal, Absolute
He begetteth not, Nor is He begotten;
And there is none like unto Him.

"Its meaning is lovely in English and its sound is lovely in Arabic," Abby said.

Just as they sat down to dinner, Matthew and Jacques knocked at the door. They came bearing a roasted turkey that was juicy and tender and delicious. Sophia wondered how it was so tender, since most of the time the turkeys they ate were a bit. . .stringy.

Matthew explained that this was one of his flock of turkeys. He kept them along with his chickens. The whole family enjoyed the bird, and then Abby and Sophia took the bones out to Sadie behind the stable. When they came back, Matthew met them in the yard. He had just filled the washtub for them.

"It's a beautiful night," he said. "I wish this humidity would ease up, though. It's goin' to be hard to harvest next week if it stays this heavy."

"It doesn't feel like rain, though," offered Abby. "At least you probably won't have to delay the harvest."

"I hope you're right," he said.

Sophia had never really spoken more than a few words to Matthew before, but she was so worried about Br. Ibrahim that she had to ask. She screwed up her courage and ventured quietly, "Have you heard anything about Mr. William today, Matthew, or the Jordans?"

"No, why?"

"Mr. William was supposed to come check on me at the Reeces, since Stan and Mr. Reece are harvesting the far wheat field. But he didn't show up. Now I feel like someone ought to check on *him*."

"Well, might be they had some other kind of work for him to do. I wouldn't worry about it. Say, did you all hear about that rabble-rouser over to Lawrence, name o' Quantrill? I hear he's stirring up all manner of trouble."

Quantrill? Of Quantrill's Raid? Sophia's skin crawled. He and his band of pro-slavery Border Ruffians had sacked Lawrence—killed scores of people and almost burned the town to the ground—in. . .uh. . .Sophia realized with a start that she didn't know when. Suddenly the warm night felt cold. Had it just happened?

"I know of him," she said, exchanging a meaningful look with Abby. "He's a disgusting war criminal." *Or will be, if he's not yet.*

"Well, that's a bit strong. I just hope he doesn't come around stirring up things over here. We got enough trouble with the slavery battle as it is."

"That's for sure," agreed Sophia.

Matthew changed the subject. "I got your note about the journal. I hope you're gettin' good use out of it."

Sophia blushed in the evening air. "Yes, thank you." She thought she would die in the awkward silence that followed, until Abby rescued her by handing Matthew the tea towel that had been draped across her shoulder and asking him to dry. The two of them washed the dinner dishes while Sophia got dessert—the cornbread she'd made smothered in molasses.

When the night was quiet and the candle blown out, Sophia was alone with her thoughts at last. She prayed for Matthew. He seemed to her to be the perfect man. Kind, thoughtful, responsible and respectful (and handsome!). She felt so bad having to tell him she didn't want to begin courting, but she could see no way to even begin to tell him about her situation, especially that her faith forbade her to marry a non-Muslim. Sophia dropped off to sleep with her thoughts drifting uneasily between Matthew, Br. Ibrahim, and Clara's attitude toward Adoeet. People often referred to the "good old days" as being simpler times. Sophia was finding that 1857 could rival the 21st century for complication any day.

ABBY HAD TO STAY home the next day and help her mother stain the floors in the new house. Mr. Sampson was at the Duncans', helping with harvest preparations, and had taken Ophelia, so Sophia rode Othello to the Reeces. She was working with Clara, speaking directly to her and asking her yes or no questions, searching for any flicker of an answer, when Mr. William came to the door.

"Mr. William! *AsSalaamu Alaikum*! I was so worried about you yesterday!"

"Aw, no need to worry, Miss Sophia. Evaline took sick, and I had to step in and mind Sam."

"Is she alright?"

"Oh, yeah. She musta ate somethin' didn't agree with her, that's all. She was back and forth ta the outhouse all night." He chuckled.

"Oh, thank God! I mean, not thank God that she's sick, thank God that nothing worse happened!"

Mr. William chuckled again. "Now, Miss Sophia, I don't got much time. But you have to keep up yoah end of oah bargain. You gotta tell me how a young, white Muslimah come to be in the Territory alone?"

Sophia reached for her backpack. "Well, Brother, my story is also quite a tale. . ."

Mr. William was dubious at first. He said the same thing that Abby had: that maybe she'd hit her head and become delusional about her past. But the pictures convinced him. He marveled at them and was particularly fascinated by her cell phone.

"There really ain't no more slavery?" he asked.

"Really. In fact, you're not going to believe this, but I swear it's true. The President of the United States is black."

Br. Ibrahim was floored. "Lordy, lordy!!" he said. "I shore do wish I could go back wit' ya and see it all!"

"Yeah, me too." Sophia really did wish she could take him back home with her. To show him her world and save him from his own.

"So do ye think you's stuck here forever?" Br. Ibrahim voiced her own perpetual question.

"I don't know. . .I thought I might go home after Stan was stung by the yellow jackets, but I'm still here. I wonder if it doesn't have to do with Clara? When Stan was stung by the yellow jackets she started to sort of come around. She's been talking a bit, and venturing out of the cabin for more than trips to the outhouse. Maybe if she can get adjusted then I'll be transported back?"

"Only Allah knows," Mr. William offered.

"The other day when I mentioned Adoeet's tribe she spat on the ground. Why would she do that?"

"Oh, Miss Sophia, many of the Indian tribes don't get along with each other. I don't rightly know which tribe Miss Clara was wit', but I'd guess they may not'a been friendly with the Kiowas."

"I see. Maybe you're the reason I'm here?"

"Me?"

"Yes. Maybe I can help you escape?" Sophia held her breath.

"Now, Miss Sophia, don't go getting' no crazy ideas. Mrs. Duncan talked ta me 'bout runnin' once before, and I jes' cain't."

"Why not?"

"Well, I cain't leave Miss Evaline, fo' one thing. An' I cain't stay and talk anymore today, neither. I gots ta git home ta her now. She still warn't feelin' quite herself."

Sophia dug in her backpack and produced some Imodium. "Give this to her if she's still having stomach problems," she instructed him. Sophia also lent him her Qur'an and he promised to recite for her the next day, after he had practiced up a bit.

Stan arrived not too long after Mr. William

left, and, tired as he was from the harvesting, he brought a small bouquet of wildflowers. He said they were for his nurses, and blushed as he asked Sophia to make sure Abby got some of them. Then he coughed and quickly asked about Mr. William.

"He came today," Sophia told him. "He's had a remarkably difficult life."

"Well, the Jordans don't seem to be too hard on him," Stan answered in that pensive way that Sophia was beginning to respect. "'Course any time a man's not free, that's hard." Stan's thoughtful manner belied his flaming red hair.

"Did you know that the Jordans sold his wife, when she was *pregnant?*"

Before Stan could respond, Mr. Reece walked in. "Don'chu fret none, Miss Sophia," he said. "Negroes don't love the same way we do. They's kinda like animals that way. I'm sure he didn't miss her for long."

Sophia opened her mouth to protest, but Stan gave her the "stop" signal behind his pa's back. So she swallowed all her indignation and fell silent.

Stan followed her out to help her retrieve Othello from the grazing pegs where he was tied up. "Don't mind my pa," he apologized. "There's just no talkin' to him about Negroes. He acts the same way about Indians."

"Don't worry, Stan. I won't hold it against you," Sophia teased him, and started off for the Sampson place, Stan's flowers tucked safely in her saddlebag.

19

MR. WILLIAM CONTINUED TO check on Sophia and Abby about every other day. He recited the Qur'an in Arabic beautifully, and would lead Sophia in prayer. When she knew he was coming, she would wait to pray with him. During the evenings and at milking time each morning, Sophia would tell Abby about Islam, and the 21st century. When she was talking about scientific discoveries, she'd often mention that this or that fact was in the Qur'an, and she realized how many of those miracles were lost on people even two centuries ago. There was no embryology, no tectonic plate theory. The barrier between salt and fresh water hadn't been discovered, nor had the different fact that iron was sent down to Earth from space. Sophia couldn't tell what fascinated Abby more, the discoveries themselves or the fact that they were all in the Qur'an.

Mr. Sampson was busy putting the final touches on the house—the roof looked great and the whole Sampson family was feeling at home in the cozy new flatboard. Stan and Abby continued to carry on a rather distant but sweet relationship. Abby was only 14, so Stan couldn't officially ask to court her just yet, but it was very apparent, at least to Sophia, that they were headed in that direction.

The actual moving to the new house took only one morning, as there were so few furnishings in the soddy, and some of them were staying. It had been decided that as soon as the Sampsons got settled, they'd move Clara into the soddy. It would be much easier for Sophia; she wouldn't have to travel to care for her. And she'd have Abby and Mrs. Sampson around as well. Stan would visit Clara a couple of times a week (and of course would get to see Abby in the bargain).

The day they brought Clara over, Stan unloaded her rocking chair and her one satchel from the wagon, spoke to her for a few minutes, and then took off to Westport, where he was roofing a church with some other fellows. Sophia and Abby could hear him whistling as he drove away. They went in to get Clara settled—the bed, table, and bench had been left but there was an empty space where the cast iron stove had stood. It had taken five men to slide it up a ramp into the wagon and they'd had to borrow an extra team of oxen to pull the wagon across the yard. As Sophia and Abby were trying to gauge whether Clara liked her new surroundings, Matthew rode up.

"Miss Sophia, can I have a word?" he asked, his dark hair blowing in the ever-present prairie wind.

Sophia looked at Abby, whose face was suddenly concerned. Matthew's voice was urgent, anxious.

"Yes, Matthew?" Sophia said, walking out the door and up to his horse. She looked up into his face. He was out of breath and his brow was knitted together.

"Sophia, I'm going to ride out with a few fellas tonight and see if we can't put a stop to this Quantrill."

"Matthew!" Sophia was instantly panicked. "You can't do that!"

"I have to, Miss Sophia. I am afraid that trouble is coming to the territory, and I want to try and head it off by getting rid of Quantrill and his ilk."

Sophia's mind flew. . .what if Matthew found Quantrill and killed him? That would alter the course of history drastically. Worse, what if he rode out now and Quantrill killed him? *Ya Allah!* What if that's what happened the first time? Was Matthew just another one of Quantrill's unfortunate victims? What if history were about to repeat itself? *Maybe THIS is why I'm here!* Sophia looked at Matthew with all the strength and stubbornness she could muster.

"Matthew, don't ride out tonight. It's wrong. I feel it. Something will go dreadfully wrong. I know about these things. Please trust me. Don't go."

For a moment, Matthew wavered. Then he frowned and seemed to sit up straighter in his saddle.

"I have to, Miss Sophia. But I'll come back, I promise. That ol' rattler doesn't have any idea we're coming. We're gonna surprise him in his skivvies tonight after dark."

"But what if you don't come back? What if he kills you?" *When was the sacking of Lawrence?! Was it before the war or during the war?* She racked her brains but still couldn't remember.

Matthew interrupted her thoughts. "I have to come back, Miss Sophia. Else how can I ask Mr. Sampson for your hand tomorrow?" With that he wheeled his horse around, kicked it into motion, and was off, leaving Sophia opened-mouthed in his wake. She stood there awhile, until Abby came up behind her.

"What did he say, Sophia?" she asked. Sophia wished Stan were still around, then she could ask him to try and talk some sense into Matthew. But Stan was long gone and Mr. Sampson was off with the Kerkhoffs, finishing up the last of their harvest.

Sophia turned her ashen face to Abby. She didn't know which piece of news was more shocking. "He said he's going to fight Quantrill tonight!" she blurted out. "And he said he's going to propose to me!"

"What?" asked Abby, responding to both

assertions at once.

"He said he and some other guys are going to go surprise Quantrill tonight and try to kill him. Then he said he was going to ask your pa for my hand in marriage tomorrow!"

"Oh, my God!" gasped Abby, again to both pieces of information. "Who's Quantrill?"

"Abby, you can't imagine what kind of guy he is. He is pure evil. He will eventually attack Lawrence and burn the town almost completely to the ground!"

"Oh, my Lord! When?"

"I can't remember! But the point is that obviously he will live. At least he did the first time. He won't be killed tonight. Which means he'll probably kill Matthew!" Then Sophia had a thought. "Unless. . .unless *this* is the reason I'm here—to have Matthew kill Quantrill so he can't sack Lawrence! Yes, maybe that's it! Except that it wasn't me who influenced Matthew to go after him. . . Oh, Abby! No matter which way it turns out, this is bad!"

"Why? I can't imagine one lone man winning a fight against a whole group of men on horseback, in the dark. If he kills Quantrill, or even if he doesn't, then he'll propose tomorrow and you could get engaged! That wouldn't be so bad! Surely if you're engaged to him then courting would be acceptable, right?"

"Somehow, I don't think that's how it's going to

happen. But even if it does, I told you, I can't marry Matthew Collins. He's not a Muslim!"

"Sophia, just relax. Whatever is going to happen to Matthew is in God's hands. Isn't that what you taught me?"

"Yes," Sophia admitted. "You're right. But what if history is going to be rewritten??" She went inside and made *wudu*, ablutions, trying to let the cool water soothe her heart. It didn't help. She begged God to protect Matthew. Nothing more— just let him live.

That afternoon lasted forever. Sophia considered asking Mr. Sampson to talk with Matthew, but decided he might want to join him instead of talking him out of it, so she kept her mouth shut. The evening was close and humid, and a thunderstorm blew in about sunset. It hung around a while, and Sophia was thankful for the new house. No water pans to mess with, no mud on the floor. They brought Clara up to the new house and she slept in the old trundle bed, which was now stored under Abby and Sophia's new bed. The girls lay in the large frame bed (which felt even larger because Joshua was in his own bed, across the room) and listened to the rain hit the glass window and Stan's wooden shingles overhead. The sounds of the storm were louder than they had been in the soddy. Sophia imagined each thunderclap as a gunshot, and prayed for Matthew.

In the morning she found out what had

happened. Matthew came over after breakfast and found the girls at the frame house. He said that he and about seven other men had ridden to Lawrence. One of them knew Quantrill's house, and they surrounded it, demanding that he leave Lawrence or face their method of eviction. After a standoff, where he did indeed come out of his house in his skivvies, they left—because even in his underwear he was armed to the teeth. He had stood in the rain and shot straight through the storm to fell one of the men's horses. "That's a warning." He'd said. "The last one you'll get." The men decided they'd overestimated their ability to intimidate him and had given up, to fight another day.

"We decided to wait and go in again next week. We're gonna gather a few more men and barge in on him this time, instead of calling him out and giving him a chance to get ready. He's gonna have to leave the territory one way or the other. Either he goes voluntarily or he goes by way of a tree, law be damned. Excuse me, Miss Sophia."

Sophia was relieved that Matthew was safe, and glad that nothing had come of the night's adventure, but she was still brooding about the possible ramifications of all this.

"Matthew, I wish you wouldn't get involved in all this. There are many other ways to fight this fight. You can get involved in politics, you can preach, you can write, you can. . ."

"Sophia, I know you're worried. And I know that violence isn't attractive to womenfolk. But this man is a menace. He's stirrin' up lots of potential danger. I'm afraid that to leave him be would result in more violence than runnin' 'im off. He's a low-down snake. Did you know he killed someone in Illinois? Sometimes a man just has to take a stand."

Sophia looked at Matthew. His hat was in his hand, as he was standing just inside the doorway of the new house.

"I understand, Matthew. My faith teaches the same thing. That allowing tumult and oppression is worse than fighting against it." She paused. "Just be careful."

"Well, I'm not a very church-goin' man," Matthew confessed. "Some things about religion just never made sense to me. But this does." He seemed to shake off the more serious thoughts. "Well, I'm off to speak with Mr. Sampson, Sophia." He looked at her with a serious, inquiring look, and Sophia blushed back at him, looking at the floor. She had no idea what to say. While she was looking down, he donned his hat and headed out the door.

The rest of the day was full of musings for Sophia. She walked Clara back to the soddy and made sure to take her journal with her. She took the little table outside and wrote until it became too hot to sit in the sun any longer. The same old questions of why she was here and if she'd ever get home haunted her, but now new ones joined in. How could she marry Matthew? How could she not? What if she was stuck here forever with no Muslim men around? Should she stay single all her life? What would happen to the future if Matthew and his men changed the past that she knew, or even if she managed to wake Clara from her stupor? Would she maybe never be born, like in that movie *Back to the Future*? For that matter, if she stayed here and had children, what would that do to her future existence? Did her future existence matter? Sophia tried to bring up the faces of her family. The only scenes in which they had clear faces were the ones in her photographs. Except her mom. Sophia could picture her at the stove cooking, in the car driving, at her desk working. . .she missed her mom so dreadfully. They could always talk about the things that Sophia was struggling with. But here there was no one to talk to. Abby was too young to offer her any wisdom and Mr. William wasn't ever around long enough. No one else knew her situation. She was on her own. And she was about to miss the midday prayer. Sophia had to force herself to get up and make her ablutions, even in all that heat.

That evening, they ate earlier than usual, since the girls were home and Mr. Sampson wouldn't be coming in from helping the Kerkhoffs until late. Mrs. Sampson approached Sophia as they cleaned up the kitchen in the new house. It was so nice to have a real kitchen, with cabinets and a sink and a pump on the floor.

"Sophia," Mrs. Sampson began, "Matthew spoke with Mr. Sampson this morning."

Sophia's mouth went dry, but she didn't stop wiping the tin cup in her hand. "Oh?" She played dumb.

"Yes. He asked him to speak with you again about courting."

"Really?" Sophia's voice was hopeful and apprehensive at once. Maybe he hadn't mentioned marriage after all.

"Yes, dear. I'm afraid he really is smitten with you." She stopped washing dishes and turned to face Sophia, drying her hands on her apron. Her face was soft. "Joseph said he asked if perhaps your family was the kind who didn't allow serious courting until after a man had already asked for your hand. He said if that was the case then he'd like to make the formal request."

Sophia stopped wiping. "I don't know, Mrs. Sampson," she fretted. "I like Matthew and I have a lot of respect for him, but I hate to make a decision like this without my family. It's like that would mean I'm really never going to see them again. I don't know. I can't explain it."

"Oh, Sophia!" Mrs. Sampson engulfed her in a hug. "I understand. To marry Matthew would make your situation feel more permanent. You're afraid it might mean you've given up hope of returning to your own family."

Sophia was grateful yet again for Mrs. Sampson. She had insight far beyond what Sophia had realized.

"Would you like to go searching for your family? I'm sure after harvest Matthew will have a bit of time. Perhaps he could take you West to look for them."

Sophia bit her lip. "No. . .I don't know. Maybe. It's just so complicated."

"Well, if it were me I'd feel a need to have someone by me at a time like this. And Matthew sure looks like he wants to be that someone. Maybe you could talk to him about it?"

Talk to him? Yeah, right. But then Sophia suddenly came to a decision. It was indeed time to talk to him. She would tell Matthew everything. About how she'd arrived, about her faith, about her reasons for not wanting to be courted by him.

Suddenly sure of herself, Sophia asked Mrs. Sampson if she could take Ophelia. She saddled her up, just one of a long list of things foreign to her "real" life that were now second nature to her, called Abby, and the two rode off down the same dirt path they'd taken the morning of July 4th.

The girls rode along the wagon tracks through the stubbled field of Mr. Sampson's newly harvested wheat. When they were almost at "Maddy Collins'" cabin, Sophia spotted a small figure coming toward them on an adjoining trail. Matthew's cabin was only about 150 yards away. Sophia slowed Ophelia to a walk.

The figure coming toward them wasn't Matthew; he was on foot. Sophia passed the point where their trails intersected, which was the point marking the boundary between the Sampson place and Matthew's land, and shaded her eyes against the sun, low in the West, to see if she could make out who it was. To her surprise, she found it was Br. Ibrahim.

Sophia walked Ophelia back to the crossroad and waited for him to meet them. Mr. William was walking slowly, carrying a plow harness. When he arrived she greeted him.

"*AsSalaamu Alaikum*, Br. Ibrahim."

The old man glanced at Abby, behind Sophia on the horse. He knew she was in cahoots with Sophia on the rescuing plan, but was so trained to hide his faith that he was momentarily afraid to return Sophia's greeting. When Sophia assured him it was OK he replied, "*Wa Alaikum AsSalaam.* Where you ladies off to this time o' day?"

"I was on my way to talk to Matthew."

"Well, I'm returning this here harness to him. He lent it to Massa Jordan to use during the harvest. What's wrong? You don't look so good."

Sophia slid off of Ophelia's muscled back and spoke earnestly to Mr. William. She meant only to ask his advice about the marriage proposal, but she couldn't stop, and all her fears and doubts came pouring out of her. Including the biggest one. She was embarrassed for Abby to hear her, but she was beyond the ability to keep it inside anymore.

"Oh, Brother, I am so empty inside. I don't feel any faith anymore. I'm so confused. I've been telling Abby about Islam, but everything I thought I understood seems so meaningless now. The situation I'm in is not fair! There's no solution for me but to stay single forever. And look at you! Your life is even more unfair. All you've ever seen is injustice and evil!! How do you keep your faith so strong?"

Mr. William put the plow harness down and Abby joined Sophia on the ground. "Now, Miss Sophia, don't fret like this. First of all, faith ain't 'bout how a body *feel* one time or 'nother. Everyone *feels* down or scared sometimes. But that don't mean you's runnin' out o' faith. That jus' means yer faith is bein' tested. Life ain't about fai'uh or unfai'uh, 'cause we humans cain't see far enough to judge that. A horse might think it's unfai'uh that we make him wear shoes, but he don't know that without them shoes 'is hooves'd get sore and ruined. It's the same way with us an' Allah. Sometimes what looks unfai'uh is really a blessin', but we cain't see it. That's why we jes' gotta believe Allah is looking out fo' us. That's why it's called 'faith', Miss Sophia. Because sometimes ya have ta believe, and that's all ya got. Look at me. I been through lots o' times when I felt scared that maybe

Allah warn't there for me, but I come out of it knowin' that He is. And my life ain't been all bad. Oh, I's seen lots o' evil, but I's also seen lots o' love and lots o' kindness."

Sophia forgot her own woes for a moment. "When?"

"Well, my Filijee was a beautiful, kind woman, who really loved me. An' I love her. To this day."

"Yeah, but she was unjustly taken away from you!"

"Well, I's seen other people's kindness. Your Mrs. Sampson gave up her time for almost a whole winter, carin' fo them Indians what had the smallpox. And Mrs. Duncan took in Adoeet. She also offered ta hep me get to the Underground Railroad, but I told her I don' want to go, like I said."

"Why, Brother? If it were me I'd take any chance I could to leave."

"Well, Miss Sophia, it's jus' ain't that easy. I's an old man now. Shoot, I didn't think I'd live this long. I get achy when it's cold and my back gives me fits. If 'n I were to have to go all the way to Canada, hidin' in people's cellars, I don't think I'd make it. It's too cold up there for an old man like me, anyhow. Mr. Jordan wouldn't be able to run the place by hisself. An' 'sides, if 'n I left, Evaline'd be all alone. She cain't travel. Not a'tall. She can hardly git up the stai-uhs in the Jordan's house."

Sophia looked at him crossways. She didn't

think all that was enough reason to stay. Except for maybe to care for Miss Evaline.

"The thing is, Miss Sophia, the Jordans ain't all bad." He raised a hand when she started to protest. "I know you think they is, and you partly right. But they's kind people in their way. Mrs. Jordan knits baby hats an' shoes for the poor women's hospital back in Atlanta. And Mr. Jordan once gave a wagon to a young couple jes' startin' out. They's generous an' kind. They don't whip us or make us stay in cold slave quarters. Young Massa Jordan is a might kinder'n his pa was that way. Lotsa slaves got it lots worse'n I does. But Miss Sophia, the Jordans is prisoners o' they own selves—even mo' than Evaline and I is. They's sort of like Pharoah, see?"

Sophia nodded, sniffing. Abby looked at her uncomprehendingly. "Victims of their own oppression."

Br. Ibrahim nodded. "Yes, and they's the ones who'll pay for it on the Day o' Judgment. I's in a far better place than them. Even if I's miserable in this he-ah life, I'd rather be me than them. 'Cause Allah IS just. And He'll even things out on that Day."

Sophia looked at her feet. She was both ashamed of her shortsightedness and frustrated because she still felt impatient and hopeless about her future—whenever that would be! Above all else, though, she felt a sudden rush of love for the gentle old man. He had become like her own grandfather. His understanding was the only thing that saved her from feeling completely alone, and he had also reminded her that Allah was the Best of Planners. Finally, she looked up. "You're right, Brother. Thank you," she said, and before she could remind herself that he wasn't her real grandfather, she hugged him. Mr. William was startled at first but then patted her back as he would a small child.

"Don't you worry none, Miss Sophia. You know, you comin' here's done me a world o' good, too. It's good to know that this country won't always be such a mess as 'tis now."

Sophia knew that in her time the country was in an even bigger mess, just without slavery. But she didn't say that to Brother Ibrahim. She wouldn't have had a chance, even if she'd wanted to, because at that moment she noticed Matthew riding up from the other side of his cabin.

"Matthew!" she exclaimed as he reached them, "We were just coming to see you," she explained, while Mr. William picked up the plow harness. Sophia began patting Matthew's horse and craned her neck to see his face, up in the saddle.

Matthew was uncharacteristically curt. "I was on my way to tell you I spoke with Mr. Sampson this morning. It appears I didn't arrive any too soon."

"What do you mean?" Sophia had never heard him speak to anyone in this manner.

"I mean," Matthew looked at Br. Ibrahim with eyes that were suddenly cold, "it appears that this slave doesn't know his place. I saw him tryin' to have his way with you."

"What?" Sophia was so shocked she couldn't even form a coherent sentence.

"I saw him with his arms around you. And in broad daylight!"

"Matthew, no. You don't understand. Br. Ib— Mr. William has been helping me with some problems—he's a very wise man, you know—and I was just thanking him."

"You mean *you* hugged *him*?"

"Well, yeah. I know it's not proper to go around hugging men, but Mr. William is like a grandfather to me, and. . ."

"I am thoroughly disappointed in you, Sophia." Matthew informed her. The two girls looked at each other with wide eyes.

"What?" Sophia demanded, still trying to get her bearings.

"Well brought up young ladies don't spend time with negroes. No good ever came a' no slave being allowed to spend time with a woman."

"Matthew, what's wrong with you?" Sophia was confused. It was as if he'd gone mad.

"What's wrong with me? I just rode up and found my girl in the arms of a nigger."

Sophia stepped backward and stared at Matthew.

She felt as if she'd been hit in the chest with a cannonball.

"Matthew? I thought you were a decent man. An abolitionist."

"I am a decent man! That's why I want to protect you. But I'm not an abolitionist. Where'd you get that idea?"

"Well. . ..aren't you fighting against Quantrill?"

"Yeah, Quantrill and his gang of vigilantes who are goin' around freeing slaves left and right. I wouldn't bother him, except he keeps stirrin' up trouble. I don't care one way or the other if this territory is free or slave, but that doesn't mean I can abide troublemakers who are fixin' to ruin it for all of us. Nor does it mean that I take kindly to a slave getting' cozy with my girl."

Now he'd done it. The shock had worn off a bit and Sophia came charging back.

"*Your* girl! I am not your girl! And I guarantee you I will never be, now, you pathetic. . .jackass!" She was just drawing breath to *really* let him have it when Br. Ibrahim, who had until this time been standing with his head down, urged her quietly to let it lie.

"Please, Miss Sophia. Don't get worked up. This'as my fault. I know better'n to do what I done, and. . ."

"What?" Sophia was beside herself, furious and not willing to let the brother take the blame for Matthew's misplaced honor. "It is not your fault that this. . ."

"Miss Sophia, it ain't legal for me to touch you. I shouldn't've allowed it, even though I know'd you meant no harm." He looked at her with a pleading expression, and she finally got it. If she put up too much of a fuss, she'd anger Matthew more, and then it would be Br. Ibrahim who would pay the price.

But the damage was done. Matthew realized that Sophia was angry with him and placed blame where it was easiest. He interrupted their frantic discussion.

"Boy, come here." Sophia was afraid he was going to strike him. Instead he tied Br. Ibrahim's hands together with his saddle rope and put the other end around his saddle horn. He didn't say another word to Sophia, but reined his mare around toward the Jordan place and set her at a trot, forcing Br. Ibrahim to jog behind, his arms pulled out straight in front of him, the plow harness forgotten in the dust at Sophia's feet.

The girls were mortified. They jumped back onto Ophelia set out for home at a run, faster than Sophia had ever had the courage to ride before.

"Ma! Ma!" Abby yelled, out of breath, as she entered the house. Mrs. Sampson came running down the stairs, skirts held up.

"What is it?"

Sophia answered. "It's Matthew. He saw me hug Mr. William and he did not approve. Started calling him names and accusing him of trying to 'get cozy' with me. Then he tied him to his horse and went off toward the Jordans. He's going to tell them, I'm sure! Then Mr. William will be in big trouble." Before Mrs. Sampson could even digest what had happened and respond, Sophia went on. "I can't believe this! We have to stop him. We have to explain!"

Mrs. Sampson hollered to Joshua to take the cherries she was boiling for jelly off the stove. She ran to the stable and saddled Othello. Mrs. Sampson sent Abby to fetch her father on Ophelia, and she and Sophia mounted Othello together. She eased the gelding into a lope and when they both got their balance, she kicked him into a gallop.

Sophia had never been to the Jordan place. Under normal circumstances, she would have been shocked, because it was the same two-story, whitewashed farmhouse with the wrap-around porch that she and her family had passed on the way into the park to ride the bike trail that morning that felt so long ago. As it was, she merely registered this information in the back of her mind as she and Mrs. Sampson rode up and dismounted. Matthew's horse stood tied to one of the porch railings.

Sophia jumped off Othello's back and hit the ground hard. She gathered herself back up and flew to the door. She knocked with great urgency and then adjusted her bonnet, which had come loose and slid sideways during the rough ride. Mrs. Sampson tied the winded horse and joined Sophia on the porch.

After a few minutes, Mrs. Jordan came to the door. She wore an expression as pure and innocent as the driven snow. "*Authu billahi mina shaitan irrajeem*," Sophia whispered under her breath. "I seek refuge with God from Satan."

"Why, Eleanor! Sophia!" she gushed in her best southern belle accent. "It's so nice to see you. Do come in, won't you please? Evaline!" she called. "Please get us some lemonade."

Sophia couldn't see, but could hear Evaline call through the swinging kitchen door.

"Yes, Ma'am." Her voice was quiet and terse. Mrs. Jordan drew them through the entry hall and into the parlor, where Sophia saw the first real furniture she'd seen since arriving in 1857. The Jordans had a horsehair sofa, an ivory inlaid coffee table, and a harpsichord! All this Sophia took in at one glance, and then returned her attention to the woman in front of her.

She began, "Mrs. Jordan, we didn't come to drink lemonade. We came to talk with you about Mr. William." She spoke quickly, out of breath, and sounded rushed and frantic to her own ears.

"Oh, yes. Mr. Jordan and Matthew Collins are out back now taking care of him. I do hope he didn't cause you too much trouble. He's always been so well-behaved," Mrs. Jordan apologized, shaking her head.

"Taking care of him!?" Sophia's voice was rising in panic. She looked at Mrs. Sampson.

"Rayetta," Eleanor Sampson began calmly, her voice steady. "We believe there has been a misunderstanding. We'd like to see the menfolk and explain."

Mrs. Jordan moved toward the parlor door, blocking the exit with her body. "Oh, that won't be necessary. We know how to take care of these things. I assure you that William will be dealt with in a satisfactory manner. He won't be bothering you any more."

"That's just it!" Sophia cried. "We don't want him 'dealt with.' He didn't do anything wrong!"

"Oh, Sophia," Mrs. Jordan said in her most condescending tone, her hands clasped in front of her cinched waist. "These things are best handled by the menfolk. Mr. Jordan knows how to take care of William. After all, we can't have him thinking that he can get away with such familiarity with young white girls. That would never do. It's for his own good. What if next time it was with the daughter of an influential person? Why, he could be lynched!"

It was as if Eleanor Sampson came awake after a long sleep. Sophia saw the spark and fire that must have lit her face when she first came out West and attended all those abolitionist rallies. Mrs. Sampson walked past Sophia and held the southern woman by the shoulders.

"Rayetta, I cannot abide you," was all that she said. Then she walked briskly through the hall, into the kitchen, and out the back door, Mrs. Jordan and a shocked Sophia trailing behind, dumbfounded.

When Mrs. Sampson stepped onto the back porch, she paused as though floored by the sight that greeted her. She caught herself by grabbing the porch post. Matthew was standing with his hands on his hips, talking to Mr. Jordan, who had a whip in his right hand—like the one her husband used on the oxen. Mr. William—gentle, patient old man with a heart of gold—was tied to an overhead branch of a young walnut tree by his wrists, which were extended above his head. His shirt was in Mr. Jordan's left hand. Eleanor's face revealed a hatred that was not to be contained by her tiny body. Sophia and Mrs. Jordan had joined her on the porch and Mrs. Jordan was trying to take her arm and direct her back inside. Mrs. Sampson flung it aside as if Rayetta Jordan were a mere cobweb. Sophia saw Evaline watching, worried, from the kitchen window.

"Gentlemen," Mrs. Sampson addressed them in a voice that was not to be trifled with. Both men were shocked into looking up at her. "You will stop this nonsense at once. This man has done nothing wrong. I demand that you untie him."

For a moment it looked as if they would comply—as if the sheer force of her indignation would bend their limbs to do her bidding.

And then Mr. Jordan erupted in laughter. When he had composed himself, he replied, "No disrespect, Ma'am, but this here affair ain't none o' your business." His voice was a lot less refined than his wife's.

Sophia was beginning to shrink back, thinking that the men weren't going to take them seriously. But Mrs. Sampson wasn't shrinking, not one inch. "Anytime a human being is being mistreated, it is my business, Sir. Whether that please you or not. Now untie him or you will suffer the consequences."

Mr. Jordan looked at Matthew, who shrugged and backed up a step. Jordan tried another tactic.

"Ma'am, we jes protectin' your young lady there. I wouldn't beat him, but once a nigger gets too familiar with white women, they're like lions that go rogue and become man-eaters. The whip's the only thing they understand." His harsh twang was downright offensive to Sophia's ears.

"Then you'll have to whip me, too." Mrs. Sampson declared, and strode over to stand next to Mr. William, who looked at her wide-eyed.

"No, Miz Sampson. Please don't put yerself in danger. I kin take it."

Sophia jumped off the porch and stood on the other side of Br. Ibrahim. "And you'll have to beat me as well," she threatened, glaring at Matthew. "Turns out this *boy*," she spat the word, indicating Matthew with her head, "is just a pathetic bigot who's insecure about his own manhood. That's no reason Mr. William should be beaten." Matthew looked like he didn't know whether to be furious or embarrassed.

The stalemate was obvious to everyone and the moment seemed to stand still. Mrs. Jordan remained on the porch, wringing her hands, which seemed to be her usual way of handling things. Sophia was surprised she wasn't overcome with the "vapors" like the Southern women in movies. Miss Evaline watched out the window with her hand over her mouth, stunned at the scene in the Jordan's backyard.

Before anyone had time to take the confrontation a step further, Mr. Sampson and Abby rode up and came around back, where they'd heard the tense voices. As Mr. Sampson looked at his wife and his adopted daughter, he became like a dog at the end of his chain—restrained only by sheer force of self-control, which was about to snap.

"Frank. What is going on here?" he asked.

"I should ask you the same thing, Sampson. Your women barged onto my property, demanding that I untie my own slave, who's about to receive a just punishment. I think you need to control your flock a little better."

Mr. Sampson's eyes flashed steel. Sophia had never imagined he could look like that. As he spoke, his Boston breeding came out and he used 100% proper English. It made him seem far superior to Mr. Jordan. Which, in Sophia's opinion, he was, of course.

"You'd better hope I can control *myself*, Jordan. Because if you don't untie that man immediately, I'm going to shoot." As he spoke, he snaked his pistol from its holster faster than any of them could react—and waited. Matthew's rifle was in its scabbard, on his horse, tied up in front. Mr. Jordan had a pistol at his side, but Mr. Sampson had gotten the draw on him. He didn't dare reach for it. He hesitated just a second and then untied Br. Ibrahim's hands from the tree.

Mr. Sampson did not lower his weapon.

"Now," he said, "Why are you whipping this fine man?"

Matthew was the one who answered. "When I came home from the Kerkhoff 's harvest this afternoon, I found Sophia in the arms of that. . .man." He knew he'd better not use any offensive language; he was on the business end of an abolitionist's pistol.

"Did you ask them what was going on?"

"It doesn't matter! He shouldn't touch her no matter what."

"Sophia, what was going on this afternoon?" His voice didn't change when he addressed her. Sophia shrank before its frost.

"I. . .uhh. . .I had some problems. I was talking to Mr. William about them, he gave me good advice, and I told him thank you. When I thanked him, I hugged him. But I didn't mean. . ."

Mr. Sampson cut her off. "Mr. William, is that what happened?"

"Yessuh."

"Doesn't seem worth a beating to me, Frank."

"It don't matter what you think, *Mr.* Sampson. William is my property and my business. You ain't got no say in it no way. There are basic rules of propriety that must be enforced or these niggers'll walk all over you. You harebrained Northerners don't understand these things, and I'll thank you to not interfere."

Mr. William was standing with his hands free from the tree branch but still tied in front of him. "William, come here."

"What do you think you're doing?"

"What I should have done long ago. This man and Miss Evaline are coming home with me. They will stay with me until such time as you agree to either free them or pay them a fair wage. You also must guarantee that you won't ever harm or beat either of them for this or any other infraction. If you choose to become violent over this matter the entire neighborhood will answer in kind until you're either dead or run off—without William and Evaline."

Sophia couldn't read the look on Mr. William's face. If it was possible to register terror and gratitude together at once, that was what it was.

Mr. Sampson called out to Miss Evaline.

"Ma'am, you come on down here. We're taking you somewhere safe."

Miss Evaline was standing on the porch now, her apron held up to her mouth. "I don't know, Mr. Sampson, Sir. . ." she looked furtively from Mrs. Jordan to her would-be rescuers, wringing her apron between her hands.

"Come on, Evaline," Mr. William said. "I'll take care of you."

As scared as she was, Miss Evaline trusted Br. Ibrahim. And what she had just seen surely made her trust Mr. Sampson, too. She came along. Mr. Sampson gave the pistol to his wife, who held it steady as an oak while he helped Miss Evaline up onto Othello's back. Abby climbed up behind her and Mr. Sampson took back the gun.

"Now. Don't you follow us. You have until morning to think about your situation. I'll come here then and we'll discuss it." He handed the reins to Mrs. Sampson, who led Ophelia around to the front of the house, Sophia and Br. Ibrahim following. Then he backed out of the yard, went around front, and had Mrs. Sampson and Sophia mount Ophelia. The women rode home with the men trailing behind, keeping watch in case the Mr. Jordan and Matthew gave chase. They didn't. But that didn't mean they wouldn't.

When they arrived at home, Mr. Sampson asked his wife to water Othello while he called Joshua. "Ride to the Duncans as fast as you can, Josh, as quickly as possible. Tell Mr. Duncan we have an emergency, and to round up as many men as he can and get here as fast as they can." His voice was quiet but urgent. Joshua understood the tone and hopped on Ophelia with no argument. He headed off in the opposite direction from the Jordan place, glad to be trusted with such an important task.

The small party then went inside. Br. Ibrahim was apologetic.

"Mrs. Sampson, Ma'am, I'm so sorry to cause you all this trouble. Please forgive me."

"Don't you think twice about it, Mr. William," Abby's mother answered. "It is I who should apologize to you. I've known slavery was wrong, but I stopped fighting against it because I was weary and frightened. I'm glad you've woken me up."

Mr. Sampson looked at his wife with a beaming pride that said, "That's my girl!" He addressed Br. Ibrahim and Miss Evaline. "Listen, I have a trap door in the cellar. Let me show you. Eleanor, bring a candle."

They opened the double wooden cellar doors on the back side of the frame house and descended the wooden stairs into a bricked cellar. Mrs. Sampson's dried roots, home-canned vegetables and smoked meat and herbs covered most of the shelves and cabinets. The far side of the cellar was reserved for sundry items. Soap, candles, razor blades and other non-food items covered the shelves, which were not just planks, like the other shelves, but rather more like a bookcase, with a back and sides. Mr. Sampson asked Br. Ibrahim to help him move the heavy case, and when they did a hole was revealed in the solid bricks. The square hole was about three feet in diameter, and they couldn't see through it to the other side—it was dark. They all looked at Mr. Sampson. He held his hand out for the candle, and when Mrs. Sampson handed it to him, he poked it through the hole. Inside was a small room with a barrel in the middle for a makeshift table and planks of wood attached to the walls to sit or lie on.

"Joseph!" gasped Mrs. Sampson, an amazed smile on her face.

"Well, I thought it might come in handy some day," he replied, winking.

Miss Evaline and Br. Ibrahim crawled through the opening and took the candle.

"There are vent holes near ceiling, William, see? There are bricks missing.. And the side of the barrel opens. Inside are some dried plums, dried venison, and a slop jar."

"Thank you, Mr. Sampson," said Br. Ibrahim.

"Bless your heart," added Evaline, the first thing she'd said since her hesitation on the steps of the Jordans' porch.

Mrs. Sampson sent Sophia upstairs for a bucket of water and when it had been passed through the opening to their friends, Mr. Sampson replaced the bookshelf. Then they all went back upstairs. The sun was beginning to set, and Sophia was hoping the other men would arrive soon. Mr. Sampson posted his wife on the back step as lookout, and he took the porch. Soon, Joshua came riding over the prairie.

He was panting when he reined to a halt. "They're on their way," he said as he dismounted. "Mr. Duncan's roundin' them up now." Sophia was proud of him and he was obviously proud of himself. He felt like a man. He took the exhausted horse to the stable for a well-earned meal and rest. Mr. Sampson called everyone to the front porch. He became urgent again.

"I don't have a good feeling about this. I was hoping that Jordan would just let himself cool down and talk tomorrow, but I don't think he will. I think he'll ride here as soon as it's dark and try to take back what he thinks is his. We'll have to be ready." He looked at his wife. "I'm sorry, Eleanor. I shouldn't have acted so rash."

"Don't be, Joseph." She put a hand on his arm. "If standing up for what's right means we have to fight, then we shall fight the Lord's fight."

"We have only three weapons. Eleanor, you take the shotgun and I'll keep the revolvers. We'll sit here inside, by the front windows. I can't imagine they'd really get violent, but then I couldn't have imagined Matthew Collins trying to get a man beaten, either. I just hope Duncan and the others get here before Jordan does." He faced the girls. "Abby, I want you and Sophia and Joshua to go to the cellar."

Joshua began to whine, "But Paaaaa! I can take care of myself. . ."

Mr. Sampson was suddenly stern, "Joshua, there will be no debate on this matter. Go to the cellar. Now."

Joshua shuffled off with his hands in his pockets.

Sophia looked at Abby and then spoke. "Mr. Sampson, I've been hunting for several weeks now. I can even hit a prairie dog. I'd like to stay and help you here."

Mr. Sampson started to object when his wife added, "She really is a good shot, Joseph."

"Miss Sophia, I wouldn't want to tell your family that I got you killed in a standoff with slaveowners." It was more a statement than an objection at this point.

"Don't worry, Mr. Sampson. I would rather die fighting for someone's freedom than live knowing I could have helped and didn't."

"Alright, then. You take the shotgun. Wait with me by the front windows. Abby, you go downstairs. Eleanor, you go back to the back door." He handed her one of the revolvers.

When everyone was in their places, all there was to do was wait. The night was hot, but not terribly humid, despite the recent rain, and there was a comforting breeze from the west. Inside the house, Sophia listened to the locusts, which had recently begun serenading in the evenings. It was a sound she had always loved, as it heralded the last few lazy weeks of summer before the air turned brisk and clean again and school started. Now, however, the locusts made it difficult for her to listen for hoofbeats.

She shouldn't have worried. It wasn't long before Sadie pricked up her ears, ran to the edge of the yard, and began barking. She was looking expectantly toward the Jordan place. Sophia could see the faint light of a torch or torches, and she knew that the slave owner had beat Mr. Duncan and the reinforcements. This was happening too fast!

Three men reined to a stop about thirty feet from the front door. In the light of their two torches, Sophia saw Mr. Jordan and two men she didn't recognize. Matthew wasn't there. The torchlight also revealed that two of the men had pistols drawn and Sophia saw Mr. Jordan remove his rifle from its scabbard.

Mr. Jordan spoke. "Sampson, I don't know what kind of stunt you think you pulled this afternoon, but the law is on my side and I'm here to get muh property back. If you turn it over right now, there won't be any trouble. If you don't, I'll do whatever I have to ta get it."

"It's not property, Frank, it's people. And they

came with me of their own free will."

"Free will? They ain't got no free will! God didn't give 'em the sense He gave a dead rat. I have free will for them. But I didn't come here to yap about this. I came for action. You have until 10 to have my slaves on this here front porch before I start shootin'. One. . ."

"Sophia, don't shoot unless they shoot," Mr. Sampson whispered.

"Two. . ."

Mr. Sampson tried another tactic. "They're not here, Jordan. We sent 'em to a safe house."

Well, it was partially true!

Mr. Jordan was not to be stalled. "Three. . ."

Time, that unique dimension that Allah had disturbed to send Sophia to the prairie in the first place, seemed to stand still. She watched Mr. Jordan count, and watched Mr. Sampson wait. She heard the locusts and it seemed funny that life on the prairie was just going on as usual. She thought the entire community of animals and bugs should have stopped what they were doing to watch the immense drama unfolding in their midst.

Suddenly Mrs. Sampson whispered from the hall. She had posted herself by the back window. "Mr. Duncan and the men are here. I see torches about a half-mile away. I don't know how many."

Sophia breathed a sigh of relief.

But in the time it had taken Mrs. Sampson to

tell them about the men, Mr. Jordan had gotten to seven.

A fleeting thought popped up out of nowhere: *The windows! These guys are gonna break the new windows.*

"Eight. . .." Sophia readied her shotgun. "*Bismillah*" she prayed. Amazingly, she felt no fear. What she felt was hesitation. She hoped the men would get there in time, because she didn't know if she could shoot a man. Sure, she was furious about the way the Jordans treated her friends—about the entire barbaric institution of slavery—and she'd thought she was angry enough to kill. But now that that her finger was on the trigger, she was suddenly wary of the gravity of actually taking a person's life. Even a scumbag. All this flashed through her mind in an instant, and by that time Frank Jordan had reached 10.

"You asked for it, Sampson!" he shouted, and cocked his rifle. But before he could get a shot off there was a zipping sound from somewhere outside, to the left of the house.

Everyone was startled, and Mr. Jordan looked down. Then Sophia saw why: there was an arrow sticking out of his side. In the light of his torch, she saw understanding dawn on his face. He looked up into the shadows beside the house, and just as he swung his rifle in that direction another arrow flew, and another. The first one hit his hip, pinning him to his horse, and the second hit the horse of the man on his right. The horse whinnied and reared up, spooking the rest of the horses.

Mr. Jordan uttered a strong oath and reined his horse around. "Nigger lover AND Injun lover!" Sophia heard him shout as he and his men made off, their frightened horses carrying them away as fast as they could. One of them shot a couple of times toward the house and did indeed break one of the new window panes.

Sophia was amazed that Mr. Jordan could ride with two arrows in him, but ride he did, and Br. Ibrahim's "owner" disappeared into the darkness.

Sophia looked at Mr. Sampson, who was blinking back at her with an equally puzzled expression. They waited a few minutes, not sure who was out there, and not wanting to be on the receiving end of any more arrows. In a moment, a small figure strode up onto the porch. Sophia dropped the shotgun.

"Clara!"

Her dress was tied up around her waist so that it made a knee-length skirt. Her feet were bare and her braids hung triumphantly to her waist. This was the first time Sophia had ever seen Clara Reece walk with her head held high. She was elegant and graceful. Her previously sad-looking feather was stuck proudly in her hair and in her hand was the bow Josh had made.

Sophia was dumbstruck. "Clara? Wha—? How did you get here? Are you alright?"

Clara smiled.

Sophia and Mr. Sampson were still basically speechless, digesting Clara's presence, when Mr. Duncan and the others finally reached the yard.

"What happened?" asked Mr. Duncan when he saw the three of them on the porch.

Mr. Sampson recovered first. "Jordan came lookin' for William and when he got ready to shoot us, Clara here nailed 'im six ways from Sundy!" he explained, his frontier accent returning.

Sophia put her arms around Clara. "Bless you, Clara!"

Clara smiled and dipped her head in return.

Then everyone started talking at once, and Sophia took Clara inside, leaving the men to go over what had happened and decide what to do next.

Mrs. Sampson met them in the hall and enveloped Clara in a huge hug. "Oh, Clara! Bless your heart! Are you alright?" As she spoke, she guided Clara into the kitchen.

Clara nodded and sat at the new table. She laid the bow next to her, but kept the quiver, still half full with the arrows that Matthew had taught Josh how to fletch, on her back.

"Oh, Clara!" Sophia exclaimed. "You were amazing out there! What a shot!" She continued gushing about Clara's timely rescue as she bustled about, getting a cup of water for Clara from the pump.

"I have been a slave." Clara almost whispered. Her voice was small and tentative, but she was speaking English!

She had a beautiful, lilting accent. It had never occurred to Sophia that Clara could still speak in the language that was taken from her when she was kidnapped so young. She and Mrs. Sampson stared at her.

Sophia burst into a bear hug and smothered Clara with it. She didn't know what to ask first. Clara hugged her back.

"How did you get here? How did you know what was going on?" Sophia asked.

"I heard you ride in this afternoon, Sophia. There is a sound to the hoofbeats of a horse when he is afraid. . .Then I saw Joshua riding out, also very fast. I knew something was wrong, so I got Joshua's bow—I was going to trade my hair bands for it when I left; it is a very good bow—and came to the house. I've been hiding here since then."

"Why didn't you ever speak before?" Sophia couldn't contain her curiosity.

"All this time I've been sitting and rocking, because there was a great. . .heaviness in my spirit. I lost my whole world twice." Clara's voice was wispy and broke often. "The first time was when I was taken from my white family. It was horrible because I was taken by a warring tribe of Kiowas west of here—as a slave. I spent several seasons with them and they were very cruel to me. Then they attacked the People and lost the battle. I was taken as part of the winnings of war. I thought I would be treated badly again, but the People were very kind to me and I became one of them. I married last spring and have a son whose name means Sleek Otter. . ." Her voice trailed off.

"Then my white father came and stole me back. I was going to run away as soon as they brought me here, but my leg forced me to wait. While I waited, I began to remember being a very little girl. Stan carried me over a rushing creek once, and he used to make dolls for me to play with. He seemed so happy that I was back, and so lonely without his mother. I felt too sad for him to leave, and then an even greater heaviness came over me. Have you ever seen bullets when they are melted down to make new ones?"

Sophia and Mrs. Sampson were listening breathlessly to Clara's story. "Yes," Sophia was able to say, because she had seen Mr. Sampson melt down bullets from his pistol on several occasions.

"That's what I felt like. I felt like my body was too heavy to move, my blood was like those liquid bullets. I became lost somewhere inside myself, somewhere between The People and the White Man. I felt I had no identity. I was torn in two—I was two halves but no whole. I had no strength anymore.

"But Sophia isn't of one people or another, and she is strong. Watching her helped me realize that

I can be a woman of the tribe with a white family, too. I can take from the strengths of both, and I can be strong. I have to be. For my son.

"I was going to run away back to the People—I know where they are making their summer camp—but I decided that running away is not honest, not befitting a woman of the People. And my brother does not deserve to go through any more sadness."

At least Sophia now understood now why Clara hated Kiowas so much. There were so many other questions she wanted to ask her, but all that would have to wait. It was getting late and everyone was exhausted. Mrs. Sampson offered to let Clara stay in the house again but she said she preferred the soddy. She thanked her, took the bow, and walked proudly through the crowd of men on the porch.

When Clara had gone, Sophia and Mrs. Sampson went down to get Mr. William and Miss Evaline, Abby, and Josh. Joshua was proud that his bow and arrows worked, and Abby was furious that she had missed all the excitement with Clara. Mrs. Sampson made tea and it was decided that Mr. William and Miss Evaline would stay in the cellar room, Mrs. Sampson would sleep in the living room, and Mr. Sampson would alternate with Mr. Duncan in staying awake and keeping watch. There was always a chance that Jordan or his men would come back and try for a surprise attack in the night.

NO SURPRISE ATTACK CAME that night, and they found out why the next morning. Mr. Jordan had died in the night. Apparently the arrow that had hit his leg penetrated an artery, and he bled to death shortly after he arrived back at his home. Sophia wasn't sure how to feel. She had never been so near death, and had certainly not been involved in the cause of anyone's death before. But Clara put it into perspective for her. "He knew there was a chance of death when he came here. We did not take death to him, he came here for it. Now he probably realizes that what he was fighting for was evil. Too bad he did not learn that while he was still in this world."

Mr. Sampson sent word to Mrs. Jordan that if she needed anything to please let them know. He said he didn't intend for her husband to be killed, but that he had been on the verge of shooting into the Sampsons' home. They didn't really expect to hear back from her, but at least they had done their duty.

Word of the conflict and Clara's heroic stand traveled quickly through the territory, and Stan and his pa showed up soon after breakfast. Stan went straight into the soddy and hugged his sister, knowing for the first time that it really was his sister in there, after all. Sophia was touched at his display of emotion—he actually cried. Mr. Reece was awkward and distant, as usual. He tipped his hat to Clara, and then said he had to go pick up a load of hay. Whether that was true or not, Sophia couldn't guess.

Stan stayed with Clara most of the morning. The girls gave them some privacy as they reminisced and got to know each other again across the gap that had separated them all those years.

As Stan and Clara visited, Sophia spoke with Abby and Mrs. Sampson. "I have an idea," she said. The other two thought it might just work, so as soon as Stan took his leave to go finish the church roof, Sophia went to talk to Clara.

"Clara," she began, "would you be willing to take Mr. William and Miss Evaline with you when you go back to the People?"

Clara thought. "The People are noble. They do not have slaves based on skin color. But they are not safe from the White Man. The summer camp is in the north of what the White Man calls

'Nebraska Territory.' If men like Mr. Jordan attack the tribe, they might be recaptured."

"Hmmm." It was Sophia's turn to think. "How far away is the summer camp?"

"On foot, about 10 or 15 sleeps."

"Could you or someone from the People take them farther north, like to Canada?"

"Perhaps. Yes, that might work. There are other bands of the People who live in the North. They could perhaps take them. But there are also warrior tribes up North. It would not be without danger."

"Well, none of their options is without danger. Let me talk to them and see if they would like to go with you."

"It is good."

"And Clara?"

"Yes?"

"I have another question for you."

"Yes?"

"Would you take Adoeet with you, too?"

Clara looked at her. The moccasin she had been sewing as they spoke lowered slowly into her lap. "The Kiowa?"

"Yes. Clara, before you say no, just listen. He is a young boy, the same age as Abby. . ."

"Hmph. A boy Abby's age is a man."

"Well, Adoeet has had a really hard life. He lost his parents last year to the smallpox, and he himself is scarred from it and blind."

"He's. . .blind?"

"Yes. He can't see. And I think his soul is heavy, like yours was. He is also a person who has two halves, but no whole."

Clara seemed to struggle within herself. "Bring him to me."

"OK, I'll try. Will you take him?"

"I do not know. I must meet him."

Sophia knew that was probably the best she was going to get out of Clara, so she took her leave and ran to ask Mrs. Sampson to arrange for Adoeet to come for a visit. Eleanor Sampson was sure Mrs. Duncan would agree, because she had often expressed how much she wished Adoeet could be reunited with his own people. She sat down and wrote a note asking her, and sent Abby to the Duncan place with it.

Sophia descended alone into the cellar where Mr. William and Miss Evaline were still staying, just in case Frank Jordan's friends paid another visit.

Br. Ibrahim preempted her questions. "Miss Sophia, me and Miss Evaline been talkin'. We sure do appreciate all that you and the Sampson's have done for us, but we think we'd better get on back to Mrs. Jordan now."

Sophia could not believe his loyalty to the woman who had enslaved him for so many years.

"If you go back to her, she'll probably have you beaten! Or worse! She'll see you as responsible for killing her husband!"

"Well, Miss Sophia, the truth is that Missus Jordan weren't ever happy with her man. He was right nasty to her most of the time. If she does have us beat, well, we been beat before. And after that's done, she'll probably pack up and move back to Atlanta. Miss Evaline misses Georgia."

Sophia knew it was time to bring out the big guns. So far she had refrained from telling people anything about the immediate future, knowing it would probably not be constructive and might make people crazy to know such things. Of course, she also wasn't sure that the future would pan out the same way it had the first time around, seeing as how some things might have been changed. But this was urgent.

"Brother, listen. In a few short years this country will go to war. The South will try to break away, in order to protect their 'right' to maintain slavery, and the North will fight to keep them in the Union. The war will last about four or five years, and hundreds of thousands of men, women, and children will be killed."

"Well, Miss Sophia, if that's what Allah wills, then I guess we'll just deal with it at the time."

Br. Ibrahim was not understanding. Sophia didn't want to tell him the rest, but she had to convince them to go with Clara.

"Brother, it will not be safe for you to be in Atlanta," she looked down. "The entire city will be

257

burned to the ground."

Miss Evaline gasped and brought her apron to her mouth again. She looked at her friend. "Maybe we should go with the Indian girl, Will. Now that freedom's in sight I can almost taste it."

Br. Ibrahim looked at her with wide eyes. "You shore, Evie? It will be hard goin', travelin' like that."

Miss Evaline dropped her apron and looked him in the eyes in the damp, dimly lit cellar.

"My whole life been hard," she said slowly. "At least this kinda hard'll be worth it," she said. "I wants ta try."

"Alright, Miss Sophia. We'll go then."

Sophia was ecstatic and terrified for them at the same time. She suddenly had misgivings—what if she'd talked them into doing something that would cost them their lives? But she reminded herself that life and death are in the hands of Allah, just as she had taught Abby. Death comes when it is meant to and its means are just secondary.

"Alright, I'll make the arrangements with Clara. We'll have to move you out soon, before Rayetta Jordan gets her head back and hires someone to come after you."

As Sophia was pushing the heavy case of shelves back in front of the secret doorway, Abby came racing down the steps. "Adoeet is here!" she announced.

The girls and Mrs. Sampson met Mr. Duncan and Adoeet in the yard. Adoeet sat straight and unmoving, just as Sophia had seen him on the morning of the house-raising.

They took him to the soddy, and Clara met them in its little yard. The Indian boy was shocked to hear someone address him in his native tongue.

Clara asked him a few questions and he answered them, reaching out to find and touch the speaker. She shrank from his touch, but continued to address him. It hit Sophia that Clara Reece spoke at least three languages. What an amazing young woman.

"We will go together, tomorrow morning." Clara announced at the end. Great Tree—that is what his name means—wants to thank you, Mr. Duncan, and your family for taking care of him, and Mrs. Sampson for her kindness last winter as well."

SubhanAllah. And Sophia had thought he was deaf! She remembered his ever solid and serene pose, and thought how much his name suited him.

When the details of the arrangement had been worked out, it was decided that Adoeet would meet Clara and their two freed friends before dawn the next morning. Stan and Jacques would accompany them to just outside the People's summer camp, and Clara would go in alone at first. When she had explained the situation, she and her husband would come and take the travelers into the camp. Sophia looked in awe at Clara.

"Bless you, Clara. I know that was hard for you."

"He is not of those who enslaved me. He was

not even born when I was kidnapped."

"Still, he is Kiowa."

"But he survived the *Ehaomohtahe*. It may mean he has been chosen by the Great Spirit to be a medicine man. Adoeet has chosen to become one of the People. It is good."

"But will the People accept him?"

"Anyone who has survived the *Ehaomohtahe* is a blessed soul. They will accept him. Besides, I have seen that the skin someone is born into is not the only way to see him. If the People resist, I will speak to the Elders of this. I think they will agree."

Sophia was beside herself with joy. Who would have guessed that Clara, Adoeet, Mr. William, and Miss Evaline would all be on their way to freedom together?

That night was bath night, but Sophia and Abby were too tired and nervous to make the trek down to the river. They decided to worry about it the next morning, after their friends had gotten on their way. Dawn was Sophia's favorite time of day, anyway.

Before she slept, she sat outside on the porch with a candle and wrote in her journal. She felt the need to write her prayers for her friends' safety on their trip. She pondered how she had changed since her arrival, back when she was just a skittish girl who worried about everything. She felt a sense of confidence in herself and her faith that she had never really felt before. And the hard lessons she had learned about the baser sides of human nature had given her a wiser, more mature outlook. She realized that the fairness of her situation was not what mattered, but rather the decisions she made with whatever circumstances she found herself in. She felt foolish for being so infatuated with Matthew Collins. She had hardly known him! And although she could understand that he was a product of a certain environment, she wasn't prepared to put up with prejudice of any kind in her future husband. She hadn't given up on love or marriage by any stretch, but she prayed that Allah would provide her with a comfortable, natural relationship with her future partner, like the Sampsons had with each other, like the one she had seen Abby start to develop with Stan. That would be far more real and far more meaningful than a schoolgirl crush.

It seemed to Sophia that she had just barely shut her eyes when Mrs. Sampson woke her, saying that Stan and Jacques had arrived. The whole Sampson family went out to bid farewell to their friends. Mr. Duncan brought his family as well, and Sophia was glad to see Mrs. Duncan, who was crying from both happiness and sadness. As it turned out, the trip would not be as difficult on Miss Evaline as Br. Ibrahim had feared. Clara had rigged a sled-like contraption behind one of the horses. "A travois," she said.

Clara, Jacques, and Adoeet rode the horses first.

Clara offered to let Br. Ibrahim ride but he would hear none of it. He preferred to walk beside Miss Evaline's "sled".

As they said their final goodbyes, Sophia said the Muslim prayer for traveling with Br. Ibrahim, and wished them many blessings and a safe journey. She was so proud of all of them. She had no doubt that they had made the right decision. She hugged Miss Evaline, let Mr. Sampson hug Stan for her, and gave Br. Ibrahim her prayer beads to remember her by. "Oh, Miss Sophia, I most surely won't forget you. You take care now," he responded. "*Jazzak Allah Khair*." May God grant you all that is good.

When Sophia hugged Clara, she said, "God bless you Clara. Thank you for taking them. You are an amazing woman."

Clara surprised Sophia with her response. "*You* are an amazing woman. You have helped me find the meaning of my name."

Sophia looked at her, not understanding.

"The medicine man gave me a name. This is not an honor that comes to everyone. He said he saw it in a dream; that the Great Spirit Himself named me."

"What is your name?"

"Nanomone'e. Peacemaker Woman."

Sophia smiled and hugged her again. "God be with you, Nanomone'e." Out of the corner of her eye, she saw Abby give Stan a bundle. As the travelers got on their way, Sophia asked her what was in it.

"Dried meat and some raisins," Abby blushed as she replied.

When their friends were gone, Sophia and Abby felt lonely already. "Let's go to the river and take our bath," Abby suggested. The day was just being born, with a beautiful pink tinge off in the east and the tiniest of breezes swirling around them instead of the steady drone of the prairie wind that would take over later in the day.

The girls rode to the river, tied Othello and Ophelia to a tree close to the bank, and waded into the cool, flowing water. Sophia pushed off and breaststroked out a little ways. She had grown to love the river, although it had taken her awhile to brave it again after her near-drowning, and this was her favorite kind of bath. The well water took forever to heat and made the house hot if you tried to bathe in the laundry tub, which was what they did when the weather was bad or they had somewhere special to go.

Sophia luxuriated in the feeling of the water flowing gently past her, taking the dirt and her worries away with it. She walked back to where the water was waist-deep, unbraided her hair, and went under, scrubbing her scalp and letting the water free her mind. When she came up, she was momentarily blinded by the bright light. *The sun sure came up fast*, she thought as she squinted into the painful rays. Then she heard rushing water and a high, wailing sound. A siren.

Sophia knew immediately that she was back home. The rushing river didn't frighten her, though. She knew she could either grab branch from a fallen tree or ride out the rapids 'til she reached a calmer part of the river. When she dragged herself out she was dressed in her original clothes, minus shoes of course, as she had lost them in the river and, curiously, minus her backpack as well.

By the time her parents came running down the bank toward her, Sophia was sitting calmly on the bank of the river. Her head hurt and her palm was scraped, but mostly she was just excited to see her family. She returned their desperate hugs and perplexed them by giggling and cradling their faces.

WHEN KUZKO SAW SOPHIA, he shouted, "*SubhanAllah*!" Little did he know that this time, it was appropriate.

At first, she was so wrapped up in returning home, in the familiar love of her family and in readjusting to the 21st century that she didn't have much of a chance to think about the implications of her experience in 1857. Then she began to miss Abby and her family, and wasn't sure how to feel about that. She had decided her experience must have been a dream. But it was so intense – the details she remembered so vivid and crystal clear – and her feelings for her friends in 1857 so heartfelt, that she wasn't sure. And the knowledge she had gained there remained with her. She was no longer frightened of every little thing, and she even remembered how to make Johnnycakes.

Sophia wanted to tell her mom and Amani

about her dream/adventure, but it was such a huge topic that she just didn't feel comfortable sharing it yet. She wanted to digest it a bit more and do some research on the web about others who had had similar experiences.

And about William Quantrill. When she looked him up, Sophia found a topsy-turvy life. The infamous Border Ruffian that Sophia knew had sacked Lawrence was only one side of Quantrill's strange personality. As a young man, he had been a schoolteacher in Lawrence. During that time and shortly thereafter, around 1857, he ran with a pack of abolitionist vigilantes who went around freeing slaves all over Northeastern Kansas and Northwestern Missouri. This was during the summer of 1857. During one of those later outings, he sabotaged the abolitionists' efforts and the result was that several of them were killed. Thereafter he switched sides. Sophia couldn't tell if he had changed his sentiments for some reason, or if his time with the abolitionists had been some sort of elaborate double cross.

Sophia also asked her parents to take her to the Underground Railroad Museum she had seen on their way to the bike trail that fateful spring day. She was shocked when they made the turn onto the dirt road. The Jordans' house stood as solid and real as it had been in 1857. Sophia's dad stopped the car. She got out and stared at the wraparound porch in front and the walnut trees in back, which had grown into quite a stand, with stately patriarch trees and young seedlings crowded together. Sophia knew what the back would look like before she rounded the corner of the house and stood remembering the day they had taken Br. Ibrahim and Miss Evaline from Frank and Rayetta Jordan, the worried way Miss Evaline had watched the scene before her, the gall of Mr. Jordan, the disappointment she had felt at Matthew's behavior. She wanted to see if the inside was the same as she remembered, but the museum was closed. The sign out front said it had been a stop on the Underground Railroad from 1858, a year after it was built and then abandoned by southern slaveowners, until the middle of the Civil War. Sophia plucked a walnut from the ground and tucked it in her pocket. She was completely at a loss.

That night, Sophia turned the walnut over in her hand. She decided that the time had come for her to tell her mom what had happened to her. She chose a Saturday morning when Hisham was at football practice and her dad was at the Damascus Cafe with Jenan's dad, Bassam, and some of their friends. She poured some iced tea and asked her mom to join her at the kitchen table. Her mom was glad to sit down for some mother-daughter time.

Sophia had planned how she would tell her mom what had happened. It was harder this time than when she'd told Abby about being from the future, for nothing had come back with her to prove her story true. But she had decided that it really didn't matter if it was true or whether anyone believed her, because it was real to her, and she had learned a lot from it. She hoped her mom wouldn't think she was crazy, though.

Just as she started, the doorbell rang.

Sophia grabbed a scarf from the hook beside the door and opened it. On the porch was a young man who looked a bit older than she was. He was wearing a kufi—a Muslim prayer cap—and freckles were scattered across his café-au-lait colored nose.

"*AsSalaamu Alaikum*," he greeted Sophia.

"*WaAlaikum AsSalaam*."

"I'm looking for Sophia Ahmed. Does she live here?"

"I'm Sophia."

The boy smiled shyly.

"My name is Shakur Jaleel," the boy said, handing a book to Sophia. "I'm the great, great, great, great, grandson of Abigail and Stanley Reece."

Sophia looked down. The black letters on the cover of the book jumped out at her. It was her journal.

Epilogue

OPHIA'S ENTRIES ENDED ABOUT half way through the journal. She spent a lot of time reading them, especially the last one, the one she had written after Clara and the traveling party had left. Where her entries ended, she was thrilled to find updates from Abby and her family.

Dear Sophia,

March 25, 1862

Stan and I were married in December of the year you came into our lives and then disappeared. I assume you went back home. We all missed you dreadfully when you did. I hope you're having a wonderful life in the future!

I told my family where you had come from and Ma said, "I always knew her being here was a miracle." It was a good thing you left your backpack, for I had all the coins and photos to show them. We told everyone else that your family had been found and you had returned to them.

Of course, I told Stan everything, and he read the entire Qur'an that was in your backpack. Halfway through it, he took his shahadah and then I did, too. I had been wanting to become Muslim since the day you helped me understand what happened to Olivia, and the fact that Stan recognized Islam as the truth, too, gave me the courage. We've never told anyone else where you came from. It is still difficult to practice Islam here—we are still the only Muslims— but that makes our lives an important jihad.

When Stan and I married, we bought the Jordan place, which was auctioned off after Razetta Jordan packed up and returned to Atlanta in November, leaving it empty. We receive and hide slaves on their way North. So far, no one has been caught, at least not while they were with us.

Abraham Lincoln did indeed become president. Did you know about this awful war, too? We don't receive mail regularly anymore, due to the hostilities, but I did receive two letters from Br. Ibrahim and Miss Evaline. They made it safely to Canada. Last I heard, they were in Toronto.

Clara (Nanomone'e) comes to visit about every other summer. She has three children now, and her husband even came with her the last time. Apparently they are well-respected in their tribe, but there is more and more trouble between the tribe and the White Men. I pray for them all the time.

I am hoping you are well, my dear sister. I will try to keep you updated on our family and I will tell all my children about you.

Love, Abby

Dear Sophia,
September 20, 1891

Stan and I moved to Detroit several years ago. There are a lot of Muslims here and more arriving every day. We love it!

We have three children and two grandchildren (so far!) I told my children about the summer we freed the slaves, and have instructed them to tell all their descendants as well, so that if our children's children's children are still around in 2013, someone can return your journal to you.

Love, Abby

Dear Sophia

June 3, 1901

My mother left me your journal. I'm sorry to have to write that she passed away last month after falling down a flight of stairs. Allah yarhamha. She spoke of you so lovingly I feel as if I know you. I will faithfully pass your journal down to my children insha Allah. I wish I could have been there with you during that exciting summer.

Sincerely
Sumayyah Reece Raja

273

Dear Sophia,

December 13, 1918

Assalaamu Alaikum! I'm
doing my duty as a Reece
descendant, adding our
family's information to your
journal, which is looking a bit
battered by now. I am the
second son of Sumayyah and
Soraqah Raja. I run a small
restaurant here in Detroit and
am studying to become the
imam of our mosque. I am
engaged to be married in June,
insha'Allah. My brother is
away fighting in the war.

Wasalaam, Waheeb Raja

Dear Sophia,
January 17, 1966

I found your journal in the storage room of my grandfather's restaurant. I can't believe he just let it lie so long. He said I could have it if I took better care of it than he did. So I brought it back to college with me in Boston. Your story is so fascinating. I'm not sure I believe it, but just in case, here goes:

My grandfather did marry in 1918 and was promptly drafted into the army. He fought in France, along the Western front. My grandmother had a baby girl while he was away, but she died in the great flu epidemic. My grandmother almost died herself. My grandfather never had a chance to return to school. When he returned from the army, they had five more children. My mother was their youngest daughter. She married my father, a welder who works at

Ford, when she was 18. He's from Morocco, but neither of them practices Islam too much. My mom sells Avon and loves to write poetry.

I am studying to be a journalist, and should graduate this year, insha' Allah. I am engaged to be married to a girl I met in Birmingham when a bunch of us went down there for a demonstration. Her name is Sister Jamilah X. She is a member of the Nation of Islam. She is a black girl. Our family has gone from abolitionists to interracial marriages. I wish our country had come as far.

I hope I'm still alive in 2013 to meet you. If the world even survives that long.

In peace, Zaid El Maghrabi

Dear Sophia,
October 1, 1975

I am `Sister Jamilah X,´ updating your journal this time. Zaid and I did get married, and we have four daughters, Alhamdulillah. I left the Nation of Islam because they did not accept my marriage to Zaid very well. We lived in Birmingham, close to my parents, for awhile, but the white people there didn't take very kindly to our marriage, either, so we moved to California. We now live in San Francisco. It´s nice because there is a strong Muslim community here, and no one gives us a hard time about being an interracial couple.

I'll try to update again soon.

Sincerely,

Ruth El Maghrabi (Sister Jamilah X)

June 23, 1984
Dear Sophia,

My family is moving from San Francisco to Santa Clara, and I found your journal in a box of books while we were unpacking. My mom said I could make the next update. My name is Ghada El Maghrabi and I'm 17 years old. I wish so much that I could go back in time like you did. What an amazing story, subhan Allah. It's only 27 years now until you will reappear in Kansas City. I hope that I can be there insha'Allah.

Love, Ghada

278

Dear Sophia,

August 20, 2013

    Well, my mom didn't make it long enough to meet you. She married my dad, an American convert she met at the mosque in Santa Clara. I'm their only child. Mom died in 1999 of breast cancer, but before she died she told me all about this journal, and made me promise to meet you on September 20, 2013. Only one month to go. I'm going to do it even though part of me thinks it's silly, because I promised my mom. Let me tell you something about myself:

    My name is Shakur and I'm 18. We live in Aurora, Colorado now, because after my mom died, my dad was depressed and wanted a change. He studied Arabic and began practicing Islam more than he had before. My mom was always a very good Muslim, masha'Allah, and my dad is now an Arabic teacher. He's teaching at the private Islamic school I graduated from here in Aurora.

I am nervous to meet you. I can't help but wonder if this is all just a joke, and I'll show up on your doorstep to find a toothless old man living there. On the other hand, if you are real, I've come to respect you a great deal through your journal entries. I can't wait to meet you. You are one brave girl.

Your potential acquaintance, Shakur Jaleel

Arabic Glossary

MUSLIMS OFTEN USE RELIGIOUS speech in everyday thought and conversation. All Muslims, no matter what their native language, use Arabic for these phrases.

Alhamdulillah—Thank God (All thanks is due to God).

Allah—The Arabic term for God. It is a personal name and is neither masculine nor feminine. It is used by Christians, Jews, and Muslims who speak Arabic.

Allahu Akbar—God is the Greatest.

AsSalaamu alaikum—The Islamic greeting. It means "Peace be upon you."

Authu billahi mina shaitan irRajeem—I seek refuge with God from Satan, the rejected one.

Bismillah or **Bismillah irRahman irRaheem**—In the name of God or In the name of God, Most Beneficent, Most Merciful.

Astaghfirullah—God forgive me

Inna lillahi wa inna ilaihi rajaun—From God we come

and to Him we return.

La howla wa la quwwata illa billah—There is no power nor authority except with God.

La illaha il Allah—There is no god but Allah.

Masha'Allah—"Allah has willed it thus." It is another way of praising God.

Shahadah—To take *shahadah* means to proclaim that you believe there is no god but God and that Mohammad was His messenger. This is how one becomes a Muslim.

SubhanAllah—Praise God (All praise or all glorification is due to God). Muslims say this when they are amazed or impressed by something.

Tasbih—the practice of praising God in a specific way, by saying "*SubhanAllah*" 33 times, "*Alhamdulillah*" 33 times, and "*Allahu Akbar*" 33 times.

Tayamum—Muslims wash before they pray. *Tayamum* is a way to perform the ritual of washing if there is no water available.

Ya Rabbi!—Oh, my Lord!

Ya Latif!—Another term that means, "Oh, my Lord!" Literally it means, "Oh, Most Gentle One!"

1850's Glossary

Ague—(pronounced A'gyu, with the emphasis solidly on the A) Ague was used to refer to any condition (such as malaria or the flu) that manifested itself in a fever with chills and sweating.

Befuddled—confused.

Bustle—A frame or pad worn under a woman's skirt to give it extra fullness in the back.

Chiggers—This term is still used and refers to tiny insect parasites (so tiny they can't be seen without a magnifying glass) who live in grassy areas and whose bites leaves small red welts that are intensely itchy.

Circuit Pastor—A preacher who, rather than having his own church, rode around to various communities to preach in a rotating circuit. He was housed by community members as he rode along, and it was considered a great honor to host the circuit pastor at your house.

Flatboard—used to refer to a "real" farmhouse, one built of lumber and not sod or tree planks.

Kiowa—A tribe of Native Americans whose original

home may have been in what is now Montana, but who migrated to the Southwestern plains. There were some as far south as Kansas/Missouri. They were eventually forced onto reservations in Oklahoma.

Providence—a way of referring to God. It indicates the care and guidance of God.

Skivvies—men's underwear. The origin of this word is unknown and it probably didn't actually come into common usage until the early 1900's. But I like it.

Smallpox—a devastating disease that raged in Europe and caused intensely painful, blistery rashes. It was often fatal and those who lived through it bore scars and were sometimes blinded. This is where we get the term "pockmarked," which people sometimes use to refer to the surface of the moon. Smallpox was not present in the Americas, and thus no one was immune to it. When Native Americans caught it, it killed unusually high numbers of people. In an early case of biological warfare, Native Americans would sometimes be given "goodwill" blankets that the Europeans knew were contaminated with smallpox. The disease would then kill off much of the tribe.

Soddy—a type of house built out of great chunks of earth, used by pioneers on the plains where there weren't many trees to provide wood for cabins.

Recipes

JOHNNYCAKES

JOHNNYCAKES ARE, IN ESSENCE, biscuit-sized fried cornbread. One legend claims that the name comes from "Journey Cakes"—as in something you could make easily on the trail or on a ship or just about anywhere, so it was a staple for people traveling.

Ingredients
- 1 cup stoneground white corn meal 1 teaspoon salt
- 1 teaspoon sugar (optional) 1 ¼ cups boiling water

Method
- Combine corn meal, salt, and sugar.
- Stir in water until mixture is smooth (it will be thick).

- Drop by tablespoons onto a well-greased griddle, and fry over medium heat for about 6 minutes.
- Turn and cook on the other side for 5 minutes.
- For thin Johnnycakes, thin the batter with ½ cup milk or water. Serve buttered with maple syrup.

Makes 8 to 10

❦ ❦ ❦

RABBIT STEW

Ingredients

1	frozen dressed rabbit
1	large onion, cut-up
1	small green pepper, cut-up
1–2	stalks celery, sliced
2	cloves garlic, chopped
	salt and pepper
½	tsp. Oregano
1	tbsp. dried parsley
1–2	carrots, cut-up
3	tbsp. catsup or tomato paste
1	cup liquid (cider, tomato sauce, or water)
10	small russet potatoes

Method

- Marinate in buttermilk for one day in the refrigerator. This should thaw the rabbit. If it isn't completely thawed, allow to remain in fridge a bit longer.
- Brown rabbit with vegetables in hot skillet for 5–10 minutes Place rabbit and other ingredients in Crock Pot.
- Cover and cook on low 3–4 hours.

Serves 4–6

About the Author

NAJIYAH DIANA MAXFIELD was was raised on the windswept prairies of central Kansas, where she learned the values of faith, family and concern for others. Those values were reinforced when she entered Islam at age 22. Unfortunately, Americans and Muslims each tend to look at the other as people who lack those values. *Sophia's Journal* is part of Najiyah's ongoing effort to help her fellow citizens and her fellow Muslims see each other for who they really are, and to remind everyone that oppression is a common enemy we must stamp out wherever we find it.

Najiyah now lives in Canton, Michigan, where she writes, speaks, avoids Daleks and roots for the USA National Soccer Teams (men's and women's!). She is the head of publishing for Daybreak Press, edits *Discover: The Magazine for Curious Muslim Kids* and studies Islam through the Ribaat Academic Program. You can write her at najiyahmaxfield@rabata.org.

Contest

*T*he *New Day Rabata Writers Contest* offers you an opportunity to be heard. Your voice is important, your story matters, and your knowledge can make a difference. Send us your manuscript today!

Daybreak Press seeks to publish the works of previously unpublished female authors with the launch of its New Day annual writing contest.

Topics rotate yearly from poetry to fiction to nonfiction. For 2015, we will be accepting fiction submissions. The deadline for submissions is December 31 each year, and winners will be announced each March.

Grand prize – A publishing package from Daybreak Press that includes author support, professional editing services, typesetting, ISBN assignment, cover design, etc., and a cash prize of $500.00.

For more information please visit http://www.rabata.org/daybreak. We look forward to reading your stories!

About the Press

$\mathcal{D}$AYBREAK PRESS is the publishing arm of Rabata, an international organization dedicated to promoting positive cultural change through the spiritual upbringing of women by women and the revival of the female voice in scholarship. Daybreak is committed to publishing female scholars, activists, and authors in the genres of poetry, fiction and non-fiction. It sponsors the annual New Day writing contest for unpublished female authors and operates the Daybreak Bookstore in St. Paul, MN. For more information, please visit rabata.org/daybreak.

CPSIA information can be obtained at www.ICGtesting.com
Printed in the USA
BVOW02s0437220814

363779BV00001B/1/P

9 780990 625902